Ages **7-8**

Disney **LEARNING**

W9-BIT-792

Magical Adventures in Second Grade

Carson Dellosa Education
Greensboro, North Carolina

This workbook belongs to:

Disney LEARNING

Published by
Carson Dellosa Education
PO Box 35665
Greensboro, NC 27425 USA

Printed in the USA • All rights reserved.   ISBN 978-1-4838-5868-5
04-188201151

Contents

Dear Parent or Caregiver,

This workbook encourages your child to practice essential skills alongside their favorite Pixar characters. It is designed to reinforce foundational concepts learned in school and boost your child's confidence in reading, writing, and math.

Examples and Practice: Pixar characters are learning partners. They provide examples to help teach your child core concepts!

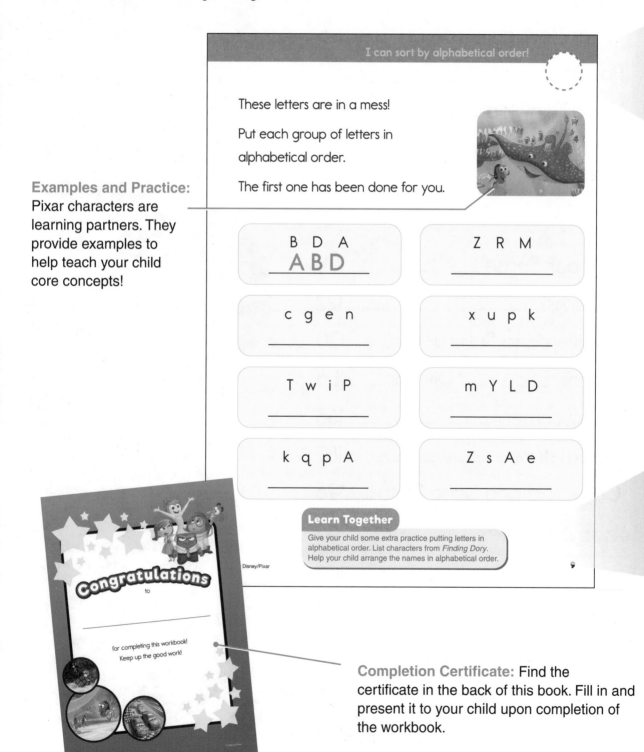

I can sort by alphabetical order!

These letters are in a mess!

Put each group of letters in alphabetical order.

The first one has been done for you.

B D A
A B D

Z R M
_____

c g e n
_____

x u p k
_____

T w i P
_____

m Y L D
_____

k q p A
_____

Z s A e
_____

Learn Together

Give your child some extra practice putting letters in alphabetical order. List characters from *Finding Dory*. Help your child arrange the names in alphabetical order.

Disney/Pixar

Congratulations

to

_____

for completing this workbook!
Keep up the good work!

Completion Certificate: Find the certificate in the back of this book. Fill in and present it to your child upon completion of the workbook.

t by alphabetical order!

r you.

I Can: Each lesson includes an "I can" statement written in child-friendly language. It indicates what your child is able to do and can also be a learning target or goal.

Reward Stickers: To conclude each lesson, a reward sticker can be placed in the dashed red circle. Find stickers in the back of this book. The reward stickers build confidence and motivate your child.

Learn Together

Give your child some extra practice alphabetical order. List characters fr Help your child arrange the names i

Learn Together: Each lesson includes suggestions for additional activities that reinforce learning. These activities promote real-world connections, critical thinking, and communication skills.

Bonus Activities: Suggestions are provided beginning on page 202 to further develop and foster your child's understanding of subject areas important to school success.

Glossary: Definitions, background information, and explanations of **black bolded** terms can be found in the glossary.

Answer Key: Sample answers for activities are provided, where necessary, at the back of the book.

Happy Learning!

Alphabet Blast Attack

The alphabet has been blasted!

What letters are missing?

Fill in the missing capital letters below.

A B C ___ E F G

H ___ J K L ___ N

O P Q ___ S T U

V ___ X Y Z

What letters are missing?

Fill in the missing lowercase letters below.

a b c d ___ f

g ___ i j k ___ m

n o ___ q r s

t ___ v w x ___ z

Learn Together

Play a game with your child: Say the alphabet, pausing randomly so your child can name a word beginning with the last letter you listed.

Clean Up
the Letters

Can Dory find her parents?

Did you notice that the words
in the above sentence are in alphabetical order?

Alphabetical order is when the letters of the alphabet are
in the correct sequence.

A B C D E F G H I J K L M N O
P Q R S T U V W X Y Z

Put these words in alphabetical order to make
another sentence.

her parents finds Dory

_____.

These letters are in a mess!

Put each group of letters in alphabetical order.

The first one has been done for you.

B D A
A B D _____

Z R M
_____

c g e n
_____

x u p k
_____

T w i P
_____

m Y L D
_____

k q p A
_____

Z s A e
_____

Learn Together

Give your child some extra practice putting letters in alphabetical order. List characters from *Finding Dory*. Help your child arrange the names in alphabetical order.

9

Alphabet Rescue!

A family saves the world.

Did you notice that the words in the above sentence are in alphabetical order?

Put these words in alphabetical order.

fast   strong   incredible

_____

robot   hero   save

_____

team   super   mask

_____

trick   defeat   mission

_____

island   secret   beat

_____

home   force   plane

_____

Learn Together

Help your child read the words and sort them into alphabetical order. Use some of these words to tell a story about the Incredibles and a mission they experience.

Missing Letters

Can you figure out which letter is missing?

_____ainbow   _____elp

_____obster   _____other

l   h   m   r

Read each word out loud.

Listen to the sound of the first letter.

Add the missing letters.

h   l   r   m

Dory ____oses ____er way.

____ow will she find the ____ight way to go?

____ost Dory ____isses ____er ____om and dad.

Read each sentence out loud.

Listen to the letter sounds.

Write your own sentence about Dory.

_____

_____

Learn Together

Help your child figure out which letter goes at the beginning of each word. Using **phonics** skills, they can try each of the letters, then sound out the word to see if it makes sense in the word or the sentence.

Who Will Win the Next Race?

Can you figure out which letter is missing?

n   s   t   w

_____eason   _____ater

_____axi   _____ighttime

Read each word out loud.

Listen to the sound of the first letter.

Draw something that begins with n, s, t, or w.

Add the missing letters.

Natalie Certain __ants __o predict the __ext __inner.

Lightning McQueen __ants __o race.

"__ime __o race!" __ays Natalie Certain.

n

s

t

w

Read each sentence out loud.

Listen to the letter sounds.

Learn Together

Help your child sound out the words and use **context** to complete the sentences. Emphasize the consonant sounds as you say each word.

Decode the Secret Messages!

Dash has received a secret message.

Decode the message for him.

___ecode this message:

___arty tonight!

___o to the ___arden ___ate.

Bring a ___ite and a ___ey.

Read the message out loud.

Listen to the letter sounds.

Add the missing letters.

____ash is faster than

a ____angaroo.

____o, ____ash, ____o!

He leaves the ____ack ____anting behind!

Those ____ids can't ____eep up.

____eople in the crowd

cheer ____ash on.

Read each sentence out loud.

Listen to the letter sounds.

Learn Together

Your child may notice that **c** and **k** can make the same sound. Talk about other letters that make the same sound (**c** and **s**).

The End of It All

It's a dark and stormy night, Woody!

Add the missing letter to the end of each word.

frigh_____   fro_____   d   m

loo_____   ma_____   t   k

Read each word out loud.

Listen to the sound of the last letter.

Add the missing letter to
the end of each word.

d   t   m   k

The toys wan___ to stay war___
on a col___, dar___ nigh___.

Do they wan___ to hide under the be___
or rea___ a boo___?

Are the friends afrai___ of the stor___?

Le___ the___ know everything will be O___.

Read each sentence out loud.

Listen to the letter sounds.

Learn Together

Help your child try each of the four letters until they find
the right one. Note that more than one letter will work on
page 18 (look, loom, loot; mat, mad). For each sentence,
they can use context to figure out the right letter.

Stop Those Evil Villains!

The Incredibles have a job to do—stopping the evil villains!

You have a job, too!

Add the missing letter to the end of each word.

p   x   f   l

bo_____   co_____

coo_____   roo_____

Read each word out loud.

Listen to the sound of the last letter.

Use one of the words to write a sentence about the Incredibles.

_____

Add the missing letter to the end of each word.

Where two letters are missing in a word, it is the same two letters.

Can the Incredibles sto___ a___ ___ o___ the evi___ villains?

Wi___ ___ they pu___ ___ o___ ___ the rescue i___ they have the right ma___?

They wi___ ___ try to foo___ Screenslaver and fi___ their car.

p

l

f

x

Read each sentence out loud.

Listen to the letter sounds.

Learn Together

Discuss how some of the words (off, pull, will) have double consonants at the end. With your child, list rhyming words for some of the words above (cop, stop, hop; cool, pool, fool). Emphasize the ending sound as you read the list over.

Happy Endings

The hermit crabs are mad. Dory needs to flee.

Add the missing letter to the end of each word.

b ˢ n g

crab___   fro___

cra___   dow___

Read each word out loud.

Listen to the sound of the last letter.

Add the missing letters.

Whe___ Dory searche___ for her family,

every cra___ trie___ to stop her.

Ca___ she find them soo___?

Dory ha___ a bi___ problem she need___
to solve!

b

s

n

g

Read each sentence out loud.

Listen to the letter sounds.

Learn Together

List other **plural words**, listening to the final letter **s** sound
(homes, rocks, helmets). Notice the **s** in homes makes the
z sound, but the **s** in rocks and helmets makes the **s** sound.

Cap or Cape?

The letter **a** can make a short vowel sound, as in **cap**.

It can also make a long vowel sound, as in **cape**. Long vowels sound like their letter names.

Say each word out loud.

Listen for the vowel sound.

Circle the words with a short vowel **a** sound.

ape   bad   rake   mask   grab

grape   Dash   race

Underline the words with a long vowel **a** sound.

apple   raid   mad   brake   cat

shake   tame   brain

The letter e can make a
short vowel sound, as in men.
It can also make a long vowel
sound, as in mean.

Circle the words with a short
vowel e sound.

bet   bee   jet   send   get

bead   feed   red

Underline the words with a long vowel e sound.

fed   beat   met   meal   meet

set   we   test

Learn Together

With your child, identify the vowel pattern or rule in some of the words
above. (When two vowels appear together in a word, the first vowel is
usually long and the second is silent, as in maid and beat.)

The Fin Is Fine

The letter i can make a
short vowel sound, as in fin.

It can also make a long vowel sound, as in fine.

Say each word out loud.

Listen for the vowel sound.

Circle the words with a short vowel i sound.

bite   bit   fine   rib

side   if   big

Underline the words with a long vowel i sound.

I   sit   write   kite   igloo

ice   it   line

The letter o can make a short vowel sound, as in not.

It can also make a long vowel sound, as in note.

Circle the words with a short vowel o sound.

boat   rock   rope   rob   robe

odd   top   mole

Underline the words with a long vowel o sound.

open   road   lock   ocean   old

soak   code   pod

Learn Together

With your child, look for patterns in these words. (A silent e at the end of a word—*robe*—makes the vowel in the middle long. Most three-letter words with a consonant, vowel, consonant have a short vowel sound—*rob*.)

© Disney/Pixar

Up, Up, and Away!

The letter u can make a short vowel sound, as in us.

It can also make a long vowel sound, as in use.

Say each word out loud.

Listen for the vowel sound.

Circle the words with a short vowel u sound.

cut   cute   but   buggy   cub

truck   sun   music

Underline the words with a long vowel u sound.

uniform   unicorn   dull   huge

unit   bug   fuse

The letter y can sometimes act as a vowel.

What letter sound does the y make in baby? _____

What letter sound does the y make in cry? _____

Say each of these words out loud.

Write the vowel sound you hear.

The first one has been done for you.

cry __i__   sky _____   try _____

lazy _____   oily _____   funny _____

The letter y can sometimes work with
a vowel to make a long vowel sound.

Say these words out loud: say they tray way

Learn Together

Discuss the vowel sounds. In the **ay** words, the **y** acts
to make the **a** long. In *they*, the **y** does not make a long
e sound. As your child's reading skills develop, they will
notice many other exceptions to general rules.

Sarge Battles R

Sometimes, other letters can make vowels sound different.

For example, in the word Sarge, a sounds different when followed by r.

The a in Sarge does not sound long or short.

The r changes the sound of the vowel.

Add the missing vowels.

m___rbles   b___rd   n___rse   f___rk

c___r   tig___r   b___rn   sk___rt

doct___r   t___rkey   w___rd

Say each word out loud.
Listen to the vowel sound.

The letter w can also change the sound of a vowel.

Read these sentences out loud.

We saw you through the window.

The jaw yawns.

Will you plow with the cow?

Take a bow, now.

Listen to the vowel sound in the blue words.

Did you notice that you don't pronounce the w on its own?

The vowel plus w makes one sound.

Learn Together

Help your child figure out the missing letters. In some cases, more than one vowel will work (burn, barn; ward, word). As you read together, look for words that follow similar patterns.

Part of the Team

Sometimes, vowels work together to change a short vowel sound into a long vowel sound.

For example, in the word team, the a helps make the e long.

Say each word out loud. Listen to the vowel sound.

Underline the two words in each row that make the same vowel sound.

sleep   mean   bait

coat   green   deal

soap   feel   boat

The letter e at the end of a word can make the vowel in the middle long.

Sam becomes same when you add a silent e.

The short vowel a sound in Sam becomes a long vowel sound.

Add an e to the end of the blue words below.

Help us us____ the remote.

Plan to make a plan____.

The cop can cop____.

Take a bit of a bit____.

Say these sentences out loud.

Listen to the vowel sounds.

Learn Together

Share the following mnemonic with your child: When two vowels go walking, the first one does the talking. Note that there are exceptions to this rule (eight, bread). Help your child make other words using a silent e.

Freezing Words

When two consonants work together in a word and you hear both letter sounds, it's called a blend.

For example, the F and r in Frozone make a blend.

Choose a **consonant blend** to make a word.

br tr sl _____ick	cl fr bl _____og
fr br sn _____eeze	fl bl cl _____ock
pl st gr _____ain	dr cr st _____eam

Violet and Dash are using spoons. What is the blend in spoon? _____

Choose a blend to make a word.

fr   tr   cl   bl   sp   sl

_____ap

_____og

_____eeze

_____ill

_____ot

_____ing

Learn Together

Your child can make a variety of words with each consonant pair and **word ending**. See **consonant blends** in the glossary for more on how consonants work together at the beginning and end of words.

Sticking Together to the End

Two or more consonants can also work together at the end of a word.

Hank is Dory's friend.

Listen to the sounds the letters nd make.

Choose one pair of consonants to make a word.

lp nt lt he_____	nt nd mp ba_____	st lp rd bi_____
st pt ct te_____	pt nt mp la_____	lf nt rd elepha_____

Choose one pair of consonants to make a word.

rd   st   nt   nd   mp

Becky is a bi_____ called a loon.

Dory mu_____ ju_____ into a drain to escape.

Dory looks differe_____ from the other fish
in the ocean.

Where will Dory's story e_____?

Read the sentences out loud.

Learn Together

Review more consonant blends (-sk, -sp, -ld, -rk).
With your child, create flash cards with a word
ending on one side and words in that **word family**
on the other side.

Sticking with Words

This is Nick Stickers. He likes bumper stickers.

When two consonants work together in a word and you hear only one sound, it is called a **digraph**.

For example, the t and h in this and the w and h in when are digraphs.

Choose one digraph to make a word.

sh th ch	sh ch th	wh wr th
_____en	_____eet	_____ale
ch th wr	th wh ch	wh sh th
_____eat	_____orn	_____ut
th ch wr	wr sh ch	sh wh th
_____ite	_____eese	_____ark

Read these bumper stickers out loud.

Underline the digraphs.

CHOOSE THE
CHASE!

Through Thick or Thin,
We Play to Win!

shape up
or
ship out

I stayed in sleepy
Radiator Springs.

Where Wishes
Come True!

Big Dreams
in the Trunk

Learn Together

Your child can make a variety of words with
digraphs such as these. List other words
with **wr** or **wh** (write, written, wrote; whale,
what, which).

Shhhh!

Buzz has hit the
mute button!

Some words have letters
that you don't pronounce.

These letters are called **silent letters**.

The letters b, g, h, k, and w are sometimes silent.

Underline the silent letters in Buzz Lightyear's name.

Say each of these words out loud.

Underline the silent letters.

thumb   sign   knock   wrist   light

comb   write   ghost   knife   right

Say each of these words out loud.

Underline the silent letters.

honest   wrist   knight   wrap   gnat

knit   lamb   character   chaos   knee

Learn Together

Create word family lists for the silent letters.
For example, record all the words your child
knows that include the letters **wr** or **kn**.

Inside Outside Words

You never know what's hiding inside!

A **compound word** is made using two smaller words.

Draw a / between the two smaller words in the word inside.

Draw a / between the two smaller words inside each word below.

The first one has been done for you.

can/not   anybody   campfire   artwork

anyone   everything   basketball   without

cupcake   sunshine   rainfall   forever

Match a word on the left to a word on the right to make a compound word.

finger   bird

home   print

humming   pack

fire   work

back   place

Circle the compound words below.

broomstick   greener   airport   jackpot

forever   jacket   sadness   daycare

Learn Together

Help your child find the little words inside bigger words when reading books together. These little words can often give clues to the meaning of the compound word.

Don't Forget, We're Supers

A **contraction** is a word that is made by joining two words.

An apostrophe takes the place of any missing letters.

Match each contraction below with the two words that have been joined.

don't	I am
we're	you are
you're	he is
I'm	do not
he's	we are

Fill in the missing contraction to complete each sentence.

___ ___ ___ ' ___ ___ about to read an amazing story.

The Incredibles ___ ___ ___ ___ ___ ' ___ had any luck lately.

They ___ ___ ___ ' ___ fly their jet.

___ ___ ' ___ broken.

An evil villain is after them. ___ ___ ___ ' ___ out to get them.

She's

can't

haven't

It's

You're

Use one of the contractions to write a sentence about Supers.

_____

Learn Together

With your child, create flash cards with a contraction on one side and the two words that form that contraction on the other. Use the cards to play matching games.

Not Again but Before

Prefixes are added to the start of a root word. Together, they make a new word with a different meaning.

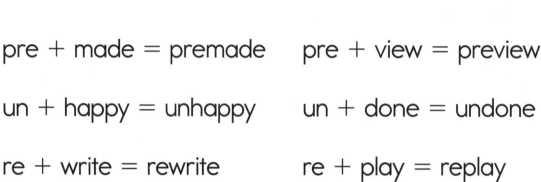

pre + made = premade   pre + view = preview

un + happy = unhappy   un + done = undone

re + write = rewrite   re + play = replay

Think about the words above. Match up each prefix below with its meaning.

pre   not

un   again

re   before

Fill in the missing prefix to complete each sentence below.

You may use each prefix more than once.

Dory is ___ ___happy when she can't find her parents.

She ___ ___visits every place she thinks they might be.

Dory is having trouble finding her parents, ___ ___fortunately.

Will her parents ever ___ ___appear?

un

re

Add a prefix to a word to make a new word.

_____ + _____ = _____

Learn Together

Help your child choose a prefix to complete each sentence.

More and Most

Suffixes are added to the end of a word
to make a new word.

For example, Lightning McQueen is big,
but Taco is bigger. Miss Fritter is the biggest.

Add the root word to its suffix.

Print the new word.

kind + er = _____

kind + est = _____

kind + ness = _____

long + er = _____

long + est = _____

Try adding -er, -est, and -ness to each of the following words.

sweet _____ _____ _____

soft _____ _____ _____

hard _____ _____ _____

Think about what each word means.

Label each wheel using small, smaller, smallest.

_____ _____ _____

Learn Together

With your child, read the words on the page. Help them work out the meaning of each word with its suffix. Encourage them to use the words in sentences.

Where to Wear Boots

Where will Woody wear his boots?

Homophones are words that sound the same, but are spelled differently and mean different things.

For example, where and wear are homophones.

Read the homophones below out loud.

Listen to how the words sound.

Think about what each word means.

eight /ate   there /their
see /sea   two /too /to

What other homophones do you know?

Use the correct homophone in each sentence.

We __ __ __ our lunch together.   ate   eight

I wonder __ __ __ __ __
Woody has gone.   wear   where

Bo Peep sees them going
over __ __ __ __ __.   there   their

What do you want __ __ do
today?   too   two   to

Why do you __ __ __ __
that cowboy hat, Woody?   where   wear

Learn Together

With your child, make homophone flash
cards. How many can you make? Use these
flash cards to create sentences.

Naming Nouns

Common nouns name general people, places, or things. **Proper nouns** name specific people, places, or things.

Read the sentences below. Underline the nouns. Then, write the nouns in the correct column.

The heroes arrive to find Syndrome waiting.

The villain snatches up Jack-Jack and races off to his jet.

The baby turns into a mini-monster in his arms.

Common Nouns	Proper Nouns

Underline the proper nouns in each sentence.

Circle the common nouns.

Mr. Incredible has strong arms that can lift boulders.

Can Dash run faster than a rocket heading to the moon?

Elastigirl can stretch her whole body around a car.

The villain reveals his evil plan as he rises into the sky over Metroville.

Learn Together

With your child, list five people, five places, and five things. Help your child make silly sentences using the items on the list (*Dad*, *kitchen*, and *spoon* can become "Dad is dancing with a spoon in the kitchen."). Ask them to identify which are proper nouns and which are common nouns.

Round Them Up!

Bo has a herd of sheep.

A **collective noun** is a word for a group of people or things. Underline the collective nouns.

A hive of bees

A class of students

A crowd of people

A pride of lions

A school of fish

Draw a lasso around the correct collective noun in the sentences.

A hive litter flock of birds landed on the house.

The herd team pride of sheep ate grass in the field.

A baseball flock team litter won the game.

Our dog had a litter school crowd of puppies.

Learn Together

Introduce your child to more collective nouns. Ask your child what their favorite animal is and find out what they are called in a group. For example; A group of bears is called a sloth, a group of zebras is called a zeal, and a group of elephants is called a parade.

Herd Those Nouns!

Bo's herded together some groups of irregular plural nouns. These plural nouns are not formed by adding **s** or **es**.

Some examples:

one calf → three calves

one woman → two women

one man → four men

one child → six children

Draw a line from each noun to its plural
form to help Bo herd them.

tooth	geese
child	sheep
goose	feet
foot	teeth
sheep	children

Learn Together

Help your child learn more irregular plural nouns. Using index cards, write
the singular form on one side and a plural form on the other. Quiz your child
with the flash cards. Some irregular plural nouns you can write on your flash
cards: person = people, foot = feet, wolf = wolves, mouse = mice.

Action!

Underline the **verbs** below.

swim   purple   play   talk   look   Dory

food   sing   ocean   laugh   eat   learn

Pick an action word.

Draw a picture of Dory doing that action.

When you add a verb to a sentence, how the verb is spelled depends on the noun it appears with. We swim fast, but she swims faster.

Underline the verbs below. Think about how the verb is spelled.

Dory sees lots of other fish in the ocean.
I see Dory.

Dory looks for her parents.
Her parents look for her, too.

Dory has a yellow tail. I have no tail.

Dory plays with her friends in the ocean.
I play with my friends at school.

Learn Together

Your child is probably already following the rules for verbs and nouns as they speak. Practice writing sentences together using a noun and verb that agree.

Action When?

Underline the verbs in the sentences below. Write them in the correct column.

Bonnie played yesterday.

Woody and Forky will be friends.

Forky dives in the trash.

Past	Present	Future

60

Some verbs don't follow the regular spelling pattern. These are called **irregular verbs**.

Underline the irregular verbs in the sentences below. Think about how the verbs are spelled.

Yesterday: The children woke up. They ate breakfast. They got on the bus. They went to school.

Today: The children wake up. They eat breakfast. They get on the bus. They go to school.

Write another sentence for yesterday using irregular verbs.

_____

Write another sentence for today using irregular verbs.

_____

Learn Together

Again, your child is probably already following these rules as they speak. As they write using various **verb tenses**, encourage them to say the sentence to figure out form and spelling. Watch out for irregular verbs.

© Disney/Pixar

Describe It!

An **adjective** is a word that describes a noun.

Riley is happy. The word happy describes Riley.

Add one of these adjectives to a sentence below.

big   friendly   blue

Riley is a __ __ __ __ __ __ __ __ girl.

Riley's eyes are __ __ __ __.

Riley has a __ __ __ problem.

Write a sentence to describe yourself.
Use an adjective.

_____

An **adverb** is a word that describes a verb.

It tells when, where, how, or what.

These are adverbs:

now, loudly, under, inside, carefully.

Riley jumps around happily.

The word happily describes how Riley is jumping.

Add each of these adverbs to a sentence below.

softly   slowly   later   outside

Riley goes ___ ___ ___ ___ ___ ___ ___ to play.

Riley walks ___ ___ ___ ___ ___ ___.

She whispers ___ ___ ___ ___ ___ ___.

Riley will be happy again ___ ___ ___ ___ ___.

Learn Together

Ask your child to describe household items using adjectives. Encourage them to consider color, shapes, smells, and textures. Give your child prompts to complete with adverbs ("The turtle moved _____." "The siren blared _____.").

A Happy, Cheerful Fish

Synonyms are words with the same or similar meanings.

Dory is a happy, cheerful fish.

Happy and cheerful are synonyms.

Draw a line to match the synonyms.

run   pretty

grin   sleepy

beautiful   jog

tired   smile

Dory needs help coming up with synonyms!
Write a new word that has the same or similar meaning as the underlined word.

Nemo <u>giggles</u> at Dory's joke. _____

Marlin is a <u>little</u> fish.

_____

Dory <u>enjoys</u> swimming. _____

The ocean is a <u>big</u> place. _____

Learn Together

Ask your child to describe themselves. Have them write the words they use, such as *funny*, *short*, or *happy*. With your child, come up with synonyms for each word such as *humorous*, *small*, or *cheerful*.

Fast and Slow, Old and New

Antonyms are words with opposite meanings.

Lightning McQueen and Mater are opposites in some ways. McQueen is fast. Mater is slow.

Fast and slow are antonyms.

Draw a line to match the antonyms.

big	last
right	never
first	wrong
always	little

Fix these sentences by coming up with antonyms! Write a new word that has the opposite meaning of the underlined word.

Cruz Ramirez is a(n) old racer. _____

Jackson Storm is nice. _____

Mater is the worst friend. _____

I hope Cruz comes in last place! _____

Learn Together

With your child, come up with a list of words to describe a favorite character. Have your child come up with an antonym for each word on the list.

Evil Robot Attacks City!

Clues in the text and picture can help you **make predictions.**

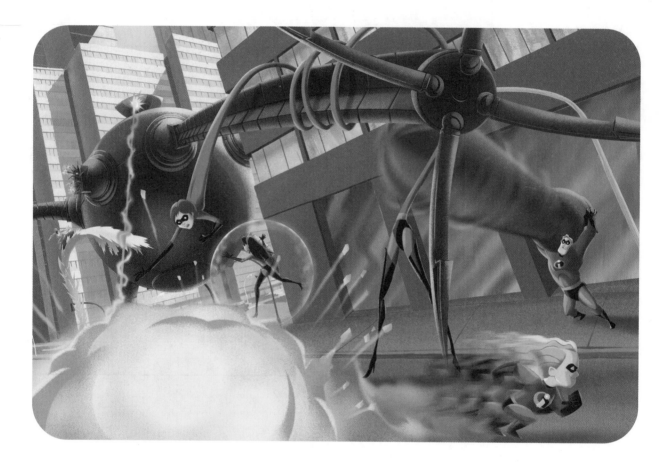

Look at the picture. Predict what the story on page 69 is about.

_____

_____ .

An evil robot is attacking the city.

The Incredibles must stop it.

Mr. Incredible knows the robot is controlled by the remote.

Frozone uses ice walls to slow down the robot.

Elastigirl aims the remote at the robot.

I'm sure that _____

will win the battle because _____

_____

_____.

Learn Together

Help your child read this story, look for clues, and make predictions. When reading other stories, encourage your child to look for clues. Before you turn a page, ask your child what they think will happen next.

That Reminds Me...

Reading stories can remind us of our own lives.

Dory forgets where her parents are.

She wants to be with them again.

Hank wants to help. He rescues Dory from the tank.

Hank helps Dory find a map.

A purple shell on the map is a clue.

Dory knows where to look next.

Underline the words in the story that remind you of something. Explain any connections you made.

_____

_____.

Learn Together

Help your child read this story. Encourage them to find different ways that a story connects to their own life. Model **making connections** ("This story reminds me of a time when I was lost ..."). Ask them questions ("Do you remember when you ... ?").

What, Where, and Who

Story elements include the plot, setting, and characters.

The plot is what happens—the problem or events in the story.

The setting is where the story happens.

The characters are who the story is about.

One day, a man steals Woody and takes him to his apartment.

Woody tries to escape. That's when he meets Jessie and Bullseye.

Jessie tells Woody that he is the star of a show called "Woody's Roundup."

Woody needs to decide: stay with his new friends or return to Andy and his old friends.

Circle the characters in this story.

Underline the setting.

Number the events in the story.

Learn Together

Help your child read this story and identify its elements. With your child, create another story. On a piece of paper, draw three boxes. In each box, your child can record ideas for the story elements: characters, setting, and plot.

What's the Big Idea?

The main idea tells what the story is about.

It can answer "who" and "what."

One day, Dory is carried away from her parents by an undertow.

Dory loses her parents for a long time.

Dory has trouble remembering things.

Dory forgets where to find her parents.

She meets her friends Nemo and Marlin.

For a while, she lives with them in a coral reef.

Finally, she remembers her parents.

What is the main idea in this story?

_____

_____.

Learn Together

Help your child read this story and identify the main idea. Start by asking who the story is about and what is going on in the story.

Picture It!

As you read, use the words in the text to make pictures in your mind.

Woody and Buzz race down the street on the remote-control car.

Woody is crouched in front, leaning over the car's bumper. His face is full of fear.

A rocket is strapped to Buzz's back. Buzz sits behind Woody, holding the remote control. Buzz has a look of concentration on his face as he works the remote.

Underline the words that help you form a picture of the scene in your mind.

Describe what you see. _____

_____

_____.

Learn Together

Cover up the image on page 76 as you read the description on this page so that your child has the opportunity to visualize the scene.

Look for the Clues

When you read, you put together the clues the author gives you. You "read between the lines" or **make inferences** to understand the text.

Bob, Helen, Violet, Dash, and Jack-Jack Parr reside in Metroville. They all have superpowers.

Unfortunately, they are not permitted to use them in public. The Parr family pretends they are like other people. Bob is bored. Dash pretends to be a slower runner.

The family is concerned other people will discover their secret. Then one day, a villain is spotted over Metroville.

How do you think the Parrs feel about not using their superpowers?

_____

_____.

I Think…Because…

When you **draw conclusions**, you are forming an **opinion** or making a decision about what you have just read. Good conclusions are based on **facts** in the text.

Riley and her family move from Minnesota to San Francisco. Riley is so sad she runs away.

Joy wants Riley to be happy. She does not want Sadness to take control because Riley will be sad.

Finally, Joy learns that she and Sadness must work together to help Riley. Joy decides that Riley needs to feel sad sometimes in order to deal with her problems.

Do you agree with Joy's decision? Why?

_____

_____

Learn Together

Talk about this story and the questions. Help your child practice drawing conclusions by talking about the characters and events in other stories ("Why did the character do that? Do you think they were right? What would you have done?").

Fact or Opinion?

When you read nonfiction, most of the text
will be facts.

Facts are what really happened or information that is true.

Sometimes, authors include opinions.

Opinions are what someone believes or thinks.

Opinions can also express a feeling.

This is a fact: Most cars have four wheels.

This is an opinion: I think all cars should be yellow.

Write **F** beside each fact and **O** beside each opinion.

_____ I think trucks are better than cars.

_____ Trucks are bigger than cars.

_____ Trucks can hold more stuff than cars.

_____ The nicest looking trucks are blue ones with big tires.

_____ Trucks are more fun to ride in than cars.

_____ Most trucks have windows.

Learn Together

Read this text to your child. With your child, write a few sentences about a topic they like (hockey, animals, music). Underline the facts. Write **O** beside any opinions. Encourage your child to support their opinions.

Tell Us About It

A title can tell you about the characters, the setting, and the plot of a story.

A title can give you hints about whether the story will be happy, sad, funny, or filled with action. What might this title tell us about the story?

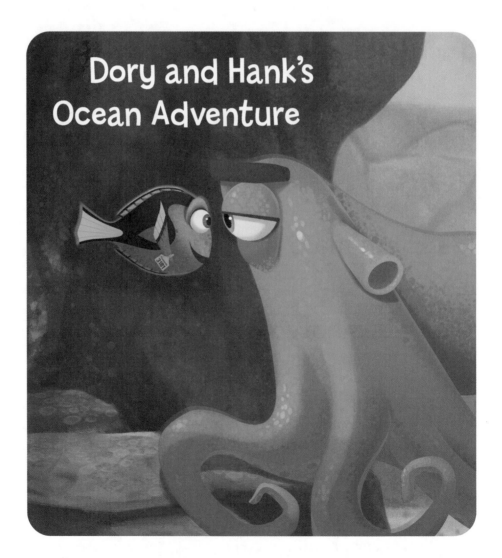

Dory and Hank's
Ocean Adventure

Think about a story you want to write.

Draw a picture for the story.

Write a title for it.

Learn Together

Discuss your child's story ideas and the title they chose. As you read stories or watch movies, discuss their titles. Point out that the first letter of each word in a title is usually a capital.

Extra Information

Labels give you extra information.

They help you understand pictures better.

Fill in the missing labels.

blue hair

Captions are sentences that tell you what is happening in a picture.

They can give you more information about the picture.

Write a caption for each picture.

_____   _____

_____   _____

_____   _____

Learn Together

Your child's labels and captions do not have to be "correct," especially if they are not familiar with this story. Check that they are accurately describing what is in the image. Provide them with family photos that they can write labels and captions for.

Sort It

Charts help you organize information.

Once the information is organized, it can be easier to read and understand.

Lightning McQueen has won eight practice races.

Cruz Ramirez has won three practice races.

Cal Weathers has won seven practice races.

Brick Yardley has won two practice races.

Create a chart with the information on page 88.

The first column has been filled for you.

Number of Practice Races Won

Lightning McQueen	Cruz Ramirez	Cal Weathers	Brick Yardley
8			

Who has won the most practice races?

_____

Who has won the fewest practice races?

_____

How many more practice races has Lightning

McQueen won than Cal Weathers ? _____

Learn Together

Help your child create a chart about a topic that
interests them. Research the information together.

Writing a Story

There are many kinds of stories.

There are funny stories and scary stories.

All stories have characters, a setting, and a plot.

What story does this picture tell?

Think about a story you want to tell.

Write your story.

_____

_____

_____

_____

_____

_____

_____

Learn Together

Your child might need help with their story before they write.
Beforehand, discuss narrative structure, how all stories need a
beginning, middle, and end. Ask about a favorite story and what
happens in the beginning, middle, and end to give them some ideas.

So True!

Facts are things that are true.

You can prove facts.

For example, Bonnie wears a green dress.

Woody wears a sheriff's badge.

Forky is made out of a spork.

Forky wants to be in the trash.

Bo is a brave toy.

Bo has three sheep friends.

Write three facts about Woody, Forky, or Bo.

1. _____

_____

_____

2. _____

_____

_____

3. _____

_____

_____

Learn Together

Your child can use the pictures to help them write facts. Or help your child research a character. List facts that your child can use to help them write complete sentences.

Capitalize That!

The names of holidays, products, and specific places need to be capitalized.

Earth Day

Fluke's Fish Flakes

Marine Life Institute

Circle the holidays, products, and places that should be capitalized.

thanksgiving   pencil

newport aquarium   dolphin

april fool's day   chum's chocolate

Rewrite the sentences with the correct capitalization.

my pet fish is from bob's fish mart.

_____

_____

i got her for christmas.

_____

_____

she loves to eat fluke's fish flakes!

_____

_____

Learn Together

Practice more capitalization with your child. Have them write the names of their favorite breakfast cereal, favorite holiday, and somewhere they'd like to go on vacation.

Writing Sentences

Sentences end in different types of punctuation.

Bob Parr is bored by his job.

How will Mr. Incredible defeat Syndrome?

A sentence that ends with a period is telling you something.

A sentence that ends with a question mark is asking a question.

Write a sentence about the Incredibles that ends with a period or question mark. _____

_____

The Incredibles are trapped!

Save the family, Violet!

A sentence that ends with an exclamation mark can show excitement or surprise.

An exclamation mark at the end of a sentence can also be a command.

Write a sentence about the Incredibles that ends with an exclamation mark.

_____

_____

Learn Together

With your child, take turns writing sentences about yourselves that end with different punctuation marks. Remind them to use a capital letter at the beginning of each sentence.

A Small Pause

Commas are used to show pauses in sentences. This is a comma: ,

After the race, Cruz Ramirez celebrates.

Lightning McQueen needs to be a better racer, so Cruz Ramirez becomes his trainer.

Commas can also show a list of items.

Lightning McQueen is fast, sleek, and confident.

Rewrite the sentences below and add the missing commas.

I like to eat cereal apples and toast.

_____

After eating I brush my teeth.

_____

If you ride a bike you should wear a helmet.

_____

My favorite colors are orange red and purple.

_____

Learn Together

Help your child write a letter to their favorite character. With your child, review sentences in the letter, looking for opportunities to include commas or other punctuation they are learning about.

Belonging and More

An apostrophe can be used to show possession.

This is an apostrophe: ´

Nemo is Marlin's son.

Dory's friends are Marlin, Nemo, Hank, Destiny, and Bailey.

Add an apostrophe to each sentence.

Dory s parents set out shell trails.

Hank s arms are really long.

A contraction is two words put together.

The missing letters are replaced by an apostrophe.

For example, is not becomes isn't.

Make contractions with the words below, adding an apostrophe.

I have _____   we will _____

we are _____   they have _____

let us _____   you are _____

he is _____   she is _____

should not _____   would not _____

Learn Together

Help your child list more contractions. Look for contractions in a story. Have your child point them out and say the two words that make the contraction.

Say It

Quotation marks show that someone is speaking.

These are quotation marks: " "

These marks are often used with the words
said or asked.

"Why would they change
math?" Bob asks.

"All over Doozledorf,
Doozles are dozing, "
Bob reads.

Look at the picture on the left. Write what Dash's
reply might be. Use quotation marks.

_____

_____

Write a story about a time you played with a friend.

What did you say to each other?

Use quotation marks.

_____

_____

_____

_____

_____

_____

Learn Together

Look at family photos with your child. Imagine the people in the photos are having conversations. Write what they're saying using quotation marks.

Speed Counts

How fast can Lightning McQueen go?

Count forward using these **number lines**.

Print the missing numbers.

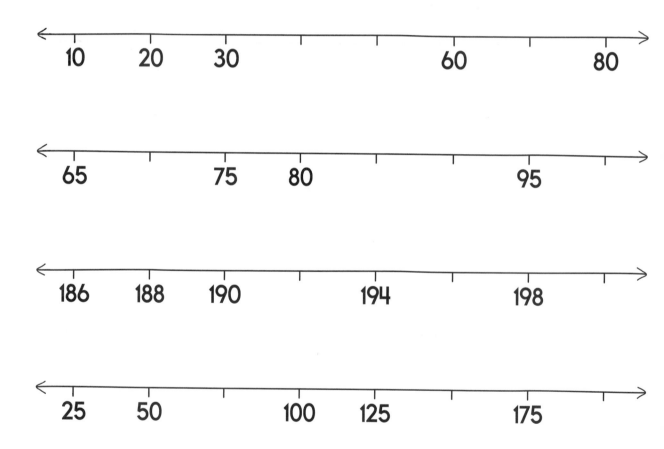

10   20   30   60   80

65   75   80   95

186   188   190   194   198

25   50   100   125   175

Print the missing numbers on the **100-chart**.

100	101	102		104	105	106		108	109
110	111	112		114	115	116	117	118	119
120		122	123	124	125	126	127	128	129
	131	132	133	134	135	136	137	138	139
140	141	142	143	144	145	146	147	148	149
150	151	152	153		155	156	157	158	159
160	161	162	163	164	165	166		168	169
170	171	172	173	174	175	176	177	178	
180	181	182	183	184	185		187	188	189
190	191	192	193	194	195	196	197	198	

Learn Together

Find opportunities to practice **skip counting** to 1,000, either by twos, fives, or tens. While counting, you might play hide-and-seek together, bounce a ball, or jump rope.

Countdown!

How many days will it take for Dory to find her parents?

Count backward using these number lines.

Print the missing numbers.

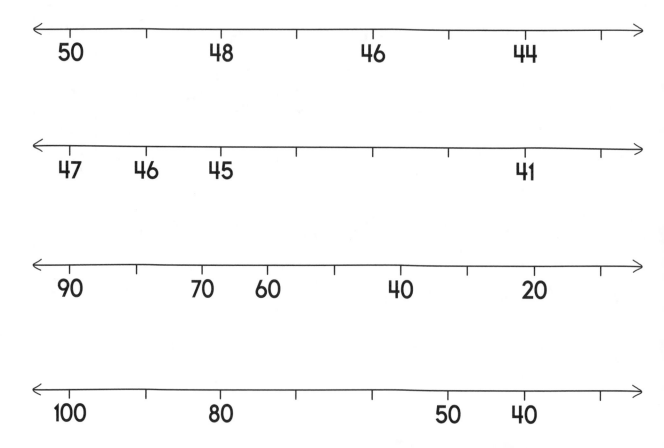

50   48   46   44

47 46 45   41

90   70 60   40   20

100   80   50 40

Print the missing numbers on the 100-chart.

100		98	97	96	95	94	93	92	91
90	89	88	87	86	85	84		82	81
80	79	78	77	76		74	73	72	71
70	69	68	67		65	64	63	62	61
60	59	58	57	56	55	54	53	52	
50	49		47	46	45	44	43	42	41
40		38	37	36	35	34	33	32	31
30	29	28	27	26	25	24	23	22	
20	19	18	17		15	14	13	12	11
10	9	8	7	6	5	4		2	1

Learn Together

Cover up numbers on the 100-chart, encouraging
your child to count backward and identify the
missing numbers. With your child, create number
lines to use for other simple problems.

Super Frames

How many blobs of goo are flying at Mr. Incredible?

Draw 23 squishy blobs of goo.

(Circle) groups of 10 blobs.

There are _____ groups of 10 blobs

with another _____ blobs.

Represent your blobs of goo in these **10-frames**.

Represent 23 another way.

Learn Together

Your child can use counters (buttons, beads) to fill the
10-frames with different amounts (25, 17, 29). Every
time they create a new arrangement, ask them to count
the groups of 10 and then say the total.

The Greatest

These racers know that order is important.

In each box, which number is greater?

Circle the greater number.

Use 10-frames to help you.

| 29 26 | 18 11 | 24 30 | 21 19 |

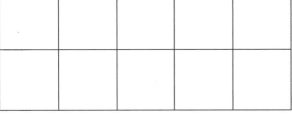

Mark each pair of numbers on the number line.

(Circle) the number that is **greater**.

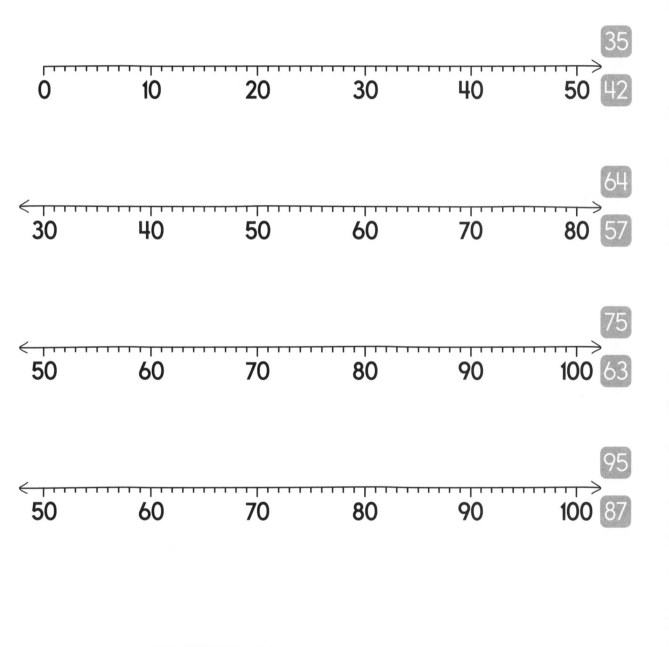

35
42

64
57

75
63

95
87

Learn Together

Use 10-frames or number lines to help your child put number sets in order from least to greatest (87, 65, 70; 82, 98, 86; 68, 83, 100). As they master sets of three, introduce a fourth number to each set.

© Disney/Pixar

Hundreds of Fans

Lightning McQueen has hundreds of fans! Figure out how many by using the flats, rods, and ones units to help you write the number. Then, write the number in its expanded form. The first one has been done for you.

2 hundreds + 1 ten + 2 ones = 212

Expanded form: 200 + 10 + 2 = 212

1 hundred + 3 tens + 5 ones

_____ + _____ + _____ = _____

Write the number!

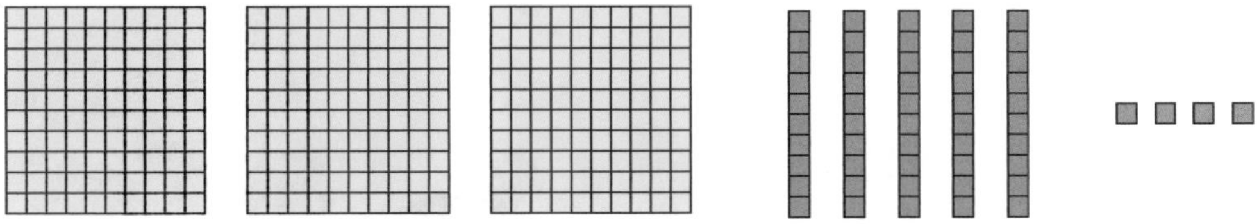

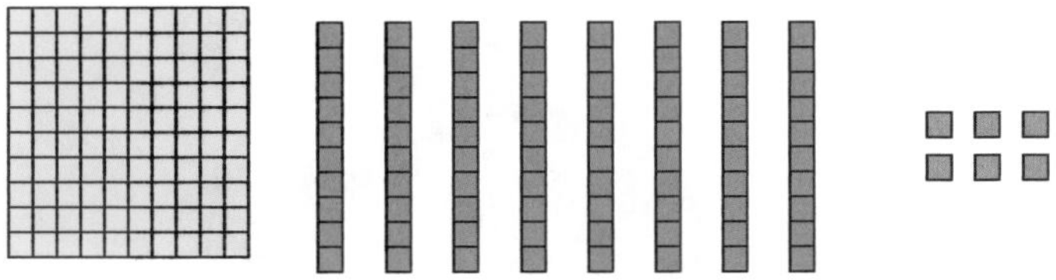

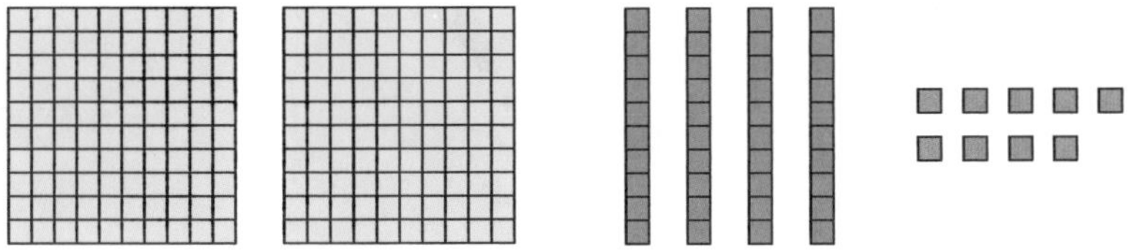

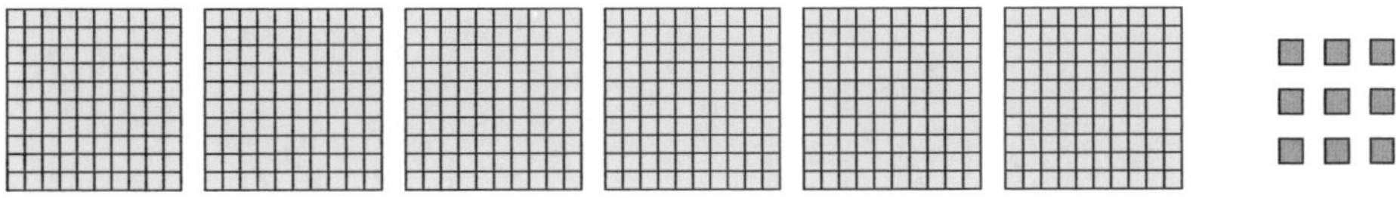

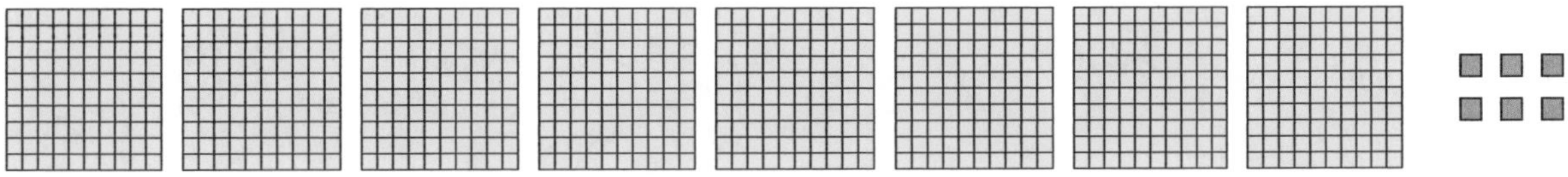

_____

_____

_____

_____

_____

© Disney/Pixar

Learn Together

With your child, go back through the answers on these pages to reinforce **place value**. Have them point to each digit in the answer and say if it is in the ones, tens, or hundreds place.

Quick Comparisons

Can you be as fast as Dash?

Write >, <, or = to compare.

460  540

157  120

575 590

918 908

837 825

432 471

551   580

742   750

912   982

220   270

118   152

366   366

600   592

884   879

755   764

178   178

448   427

912   941

Learn Together

Your child should understand that the three digits of a number represent hundreds, tens, and ones. Use the numbers on this page. Ask your child what number is in the hundreds, tens, and ones place.

We're Rich!

Woody and Buzz are counting money.

Draw a line from the money to its value.

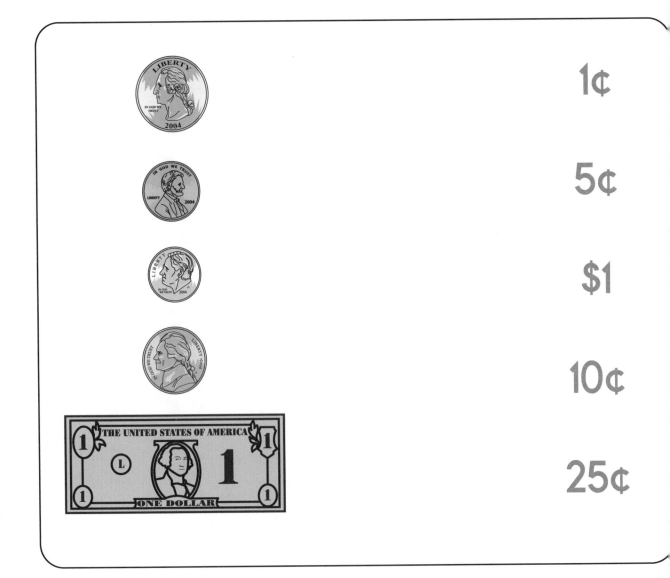

1¢

5¢

$1

10¢

25¢

Show 25¢ in 2 ways.

Show 50¢ in 2 ways.

Show $1 in 2 ways.

Learn Together

Work with your child to figure out other ways to show these amounts. Use coins to help them.

Just a Fraction

The Omnidroid can break whole objects apart!

A part of a whole is called a fraction.

When there are **2** equal parts, we call each part a half.

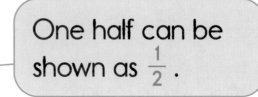

One half can be shown as $\frac{1}{2}$.

Color half of each shape below.

The first one has been done for you.

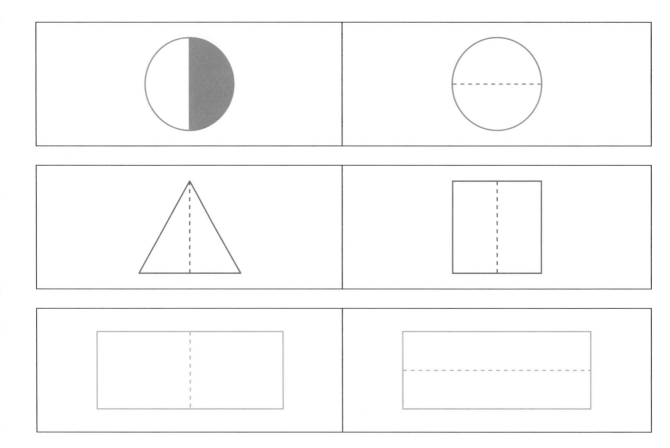

When there are 4 equal parts,

we call each part

a fourth or a quarter.

One quarter can be shown as $\frac{1}{4}$.

Color one fourth of each shape below.

The first one has been done for you.

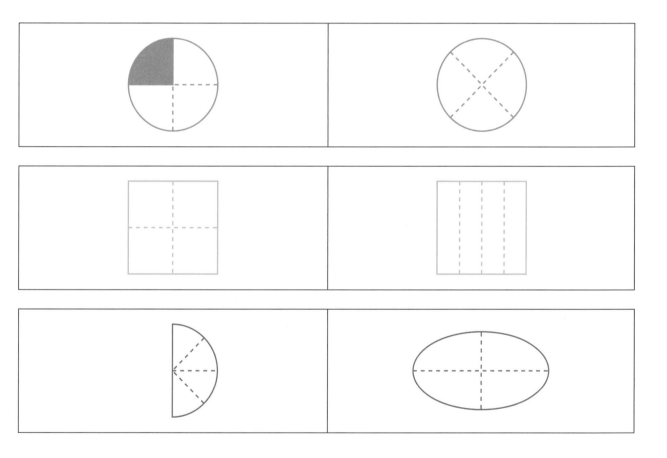

Learn Together

With your child, discuss halves and fourths when you are looking at objects, particularly food that might be shared (crackers, pizza, cake, sandwiches).

Part of a Whole

Riley and her family need to split each dish into three equal parts.

When there are 3 equal parts, we call each part a third.

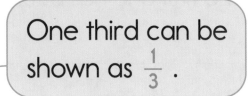

One third can be shown as $\frac{1}{3}$.

Color one third of each shape.

The first one has been done for you.

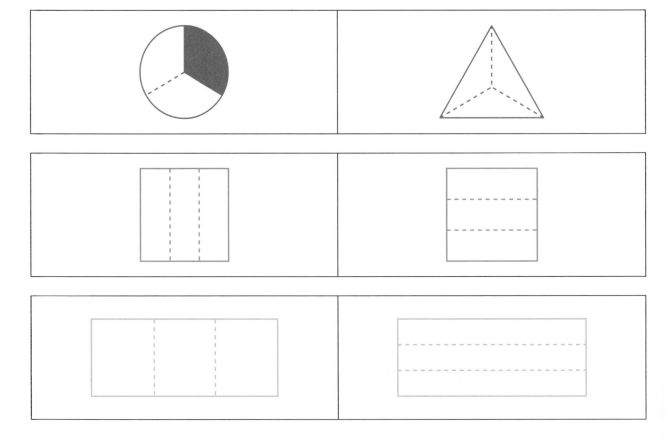

This bar is 8 blocks long.

Split the bar in half.

How many blocks are in each half? _____

This bar is 4 blocks long.

Split the bar in fourths.

How many blocks are in each fourth? _____

This bar is 9 blocks long.

Split the bar in thirds.

How many blocks are in each third? _____

Learn Together

Repeat this activity using different numbers of interlocking blocks.

Over and Over

Patterns repeat over and over. Spot the pattern in this picture.

Draw the part of each pattern that repeats over and over.

_____

_____

_____

ABA ABA ABA ABA _____

Describe one of the patterns above.

_____

Patterns can change by size, shape, color, or direction.

Draw the part of each pattern that repeats.

 _____

 _____

 _____

ABcD ABcD ABcD ABcD_____

Describe one of the patterns above.

_____

Colorful Patterns

What patterns do you see in this picture?

Finish each of the patterns below by adding color.

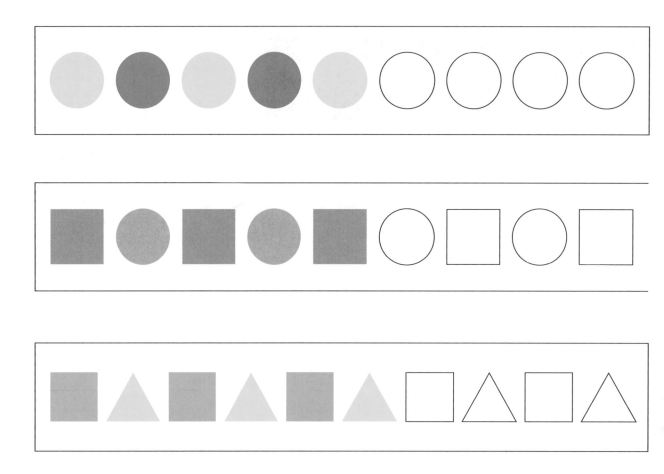

Choose 2 shapes and 2 colors to make
a pattern. Draw your pattern.

Now choose 3 shapes and 3 colors to make
a pattern. Draw your pattern.

Learn Together

Look for patterns in your home (tiles or wallpaper, or how the
table is set: fork, plate, glass, fork, plate, glass). Encourage
your child to describe the pattern and continue it.

Growing and Shrinking

Extend each pattern.

(Circle) if the pattern is shrinking or growing.

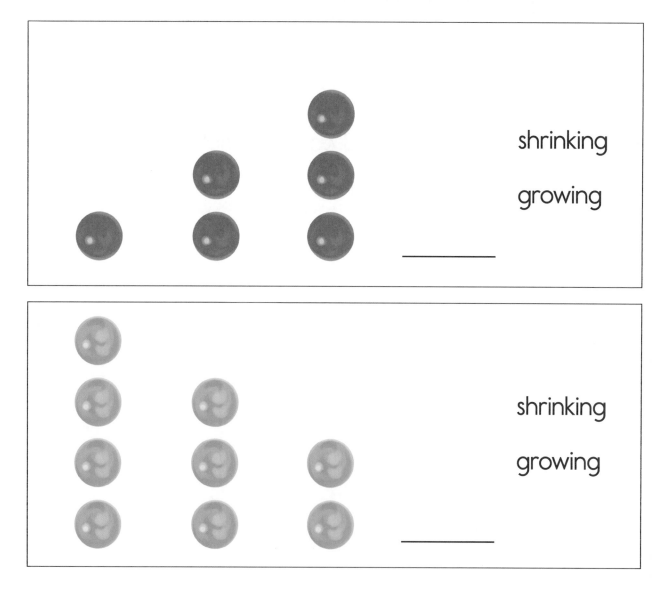

shrinking

growing

_____

shrinking

growing

_____

Extend each pattern.

Circle if the pattern is shrinking or growing.

5 10 15 20 25 30 _____

shrinking

growing

EEEEE EEEE EEE _____

shrinking

growing

32 30 28 26 24 22 _____

shrinking

growing

Learn Together

With your child, create shrinking and growing patterns for each other to extend.

Skipping Along

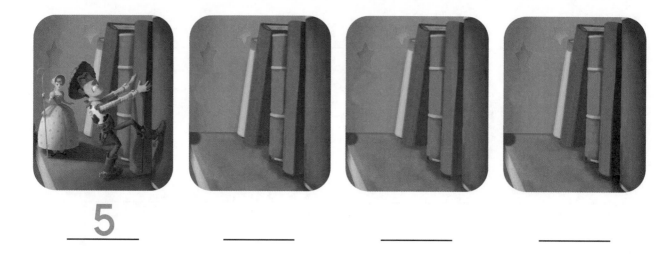

__5__ ___ ___ ___

Each bookshelf can hold 5 books.

Skip count by 5s.

How many books are there in total? _____

Hamm holds 4 quarters.

Skip count by 25s.

__25¢__ ___ ___ ___

How much money is there in total? _____

Find the next 3 numbers.

25, 30, _____ , _____ , _____

20, 30, _____ , _____ , _____

100, 200, _____ , _____ , _____

600, 700, _____ , _____ , _____

50, 60, _____ , _____ , _____

45, 50, _____ , _____ , _____

80, 90, _____ , _____ , _____

Learn Together

Make number lines of different intervals to help your child practice skip counting.

It All Adds Up

How many times do Fluke and Rudder bark at Gerald?

3 + 6 = ☐

4 + 2 = ☐

7 + 10 = ☐

9 + 9 = ☐

11 + 5 = ☐

4 + 8 = ☐

14 + 2 = ☐

Look at the 10-frames.

Write the **addition sentences**.

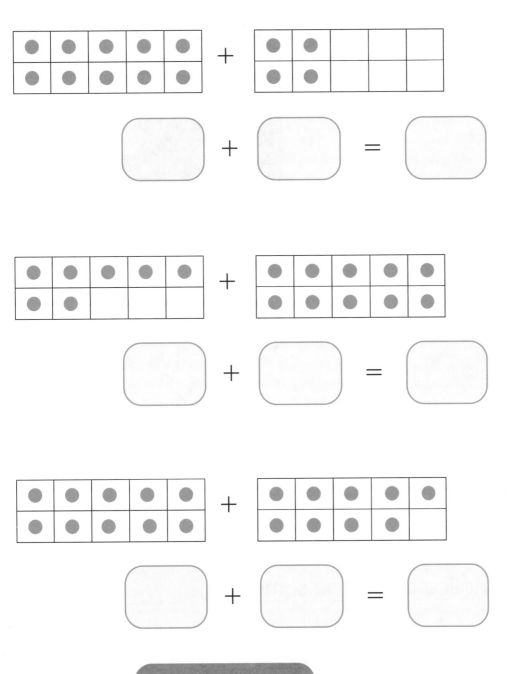

Learn Together

Use toy cars or other objects to recreate the equations on page 130. Create other problems for your child to solve using the toys. Encourage them to record the problem using an addition sentence.

© Disney/Pixar

How Many?

19 friends help Dory escape.

1 Dory and 19 friends

is

Find each sum.

$11 + 9 = $ ⬚

$6 + 14 = $ ⬚

$19 + 1 = $ ⬚

$9 + 11 = $ ⬚

What do you notice about the sums?

_____

Find each sum.

12 + 8 = ☐   15 + 5 = ☐

3 + 17 = ☐   5 + 15 = ☐

What do you notice about the sums?

_____

Write another addition sentence that fits
with the ones above.

Learn Together

Your child can use counters or objects to show the
same number in different ways (15 can be shown
using 10 counters and 5 counters, 7 counters and 8
counters, 12 counters and 3 counters, and so on).

Solve It!

The Incredibles know how to solve problems.

How do you solve two-digit addition problems?

You can solve 10 + 14 using a 50-chart.

Find 14 on the 50-chart. Jump forward 10 to get 24.

1	2	3	4	5	6	7	8	9	10
11	12	13	14	15	16	17	18	19	20
21	22	23	24	25	26	27	28	29	30
31	32	33	34	35	36	37	38	39	40
41	42	43	44	45	46	47	48	49	50

You can also solve 10 + 14 by making friendly numbers.

10 + 14

10 + 10 + 4 = 24

So, 10 + 14 = 24

Find each sum.

13 + 10 = ☐

15 + 10 = ☐

16 + 10 = ☐

17 + 10 = ☐

20 + 10 = ☐

20 + 13 = ☐

20 + 15 = ☐

20 + 20 = ☐

20 + 21 = ☐

20 + 22 = ☐

Learn Together

Your child may use various strategies to solve these problems, including using a 50-chart, interconnecting blocks, or counters on 10-frames. Discuss the strategies they are using.

Adding Three Digits

Buzz is leading this problem-solving mission. Help him solve the addition problems!

124 + 100 = ☐   500 + 133 = ☐

350 + 200 = ☐   600 + 246 = ☐

810 + 100 = ☐   416 + 310 = ☐

Keep solving!

651 + 121 = [ ]

700 + 299 = [ ]

476 + 504 = [ ]

811 + 137 = [ ]

909 + 85 = [ ]

360 + 340 = [ ]

113 + 219 = [ ]

575 + 125 = [ ]

Learn Together

Help your child with these three-digit addition problems. You can help by lining up numbers according to place value. Encourage them if they get stuck.

Add That Cash

Money is kept in cash registers.

Look at the coins.

Write addition sentences.

Figure out how much money there is in total.

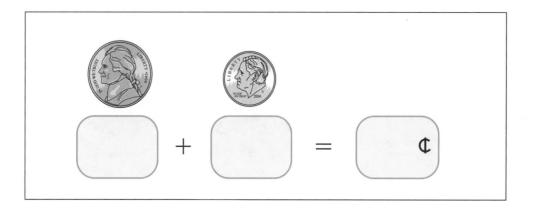

[ ] + [ ] = [ ] ¢

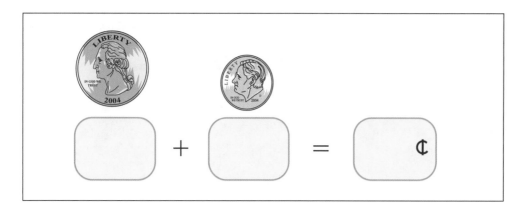

[ ] + [ ] = [ ] ¢

Look at the coins.

Estimate, then find the total.

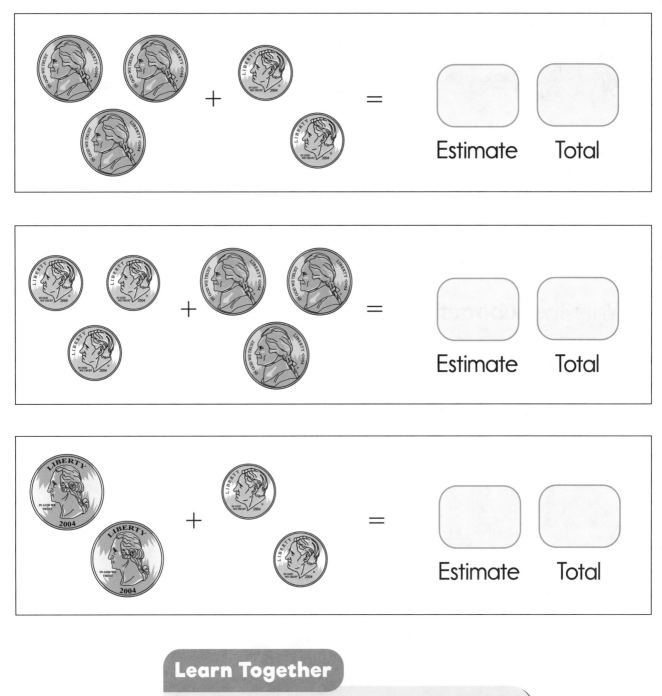

Learn Together

Your child might use real coins to help them with these addition problems. Provide them with similar problems to practice **estimating** and adding.

I "Otter" Take Some Away

There are 12 otters.

Some of the otters dive under the water.

How many are left?

Write the **subtraction sentence**.

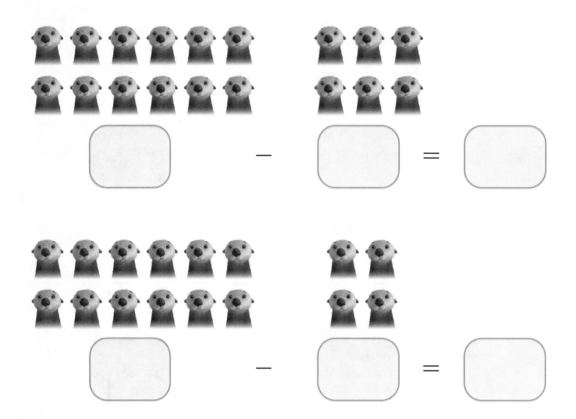

$$\boxed{} - \boxed{} = \boxed{}$$

$$\boxed{} - \boxed{} = \boxed{}$$

Look at the 10-frames.

Write the subtraction sentences.

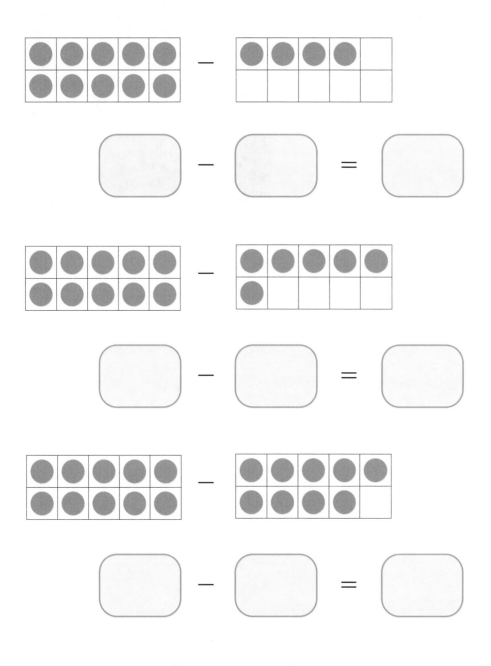

- ( ) − ( ) = ( )

- ( ) − ( ) = ( )

- ( ) − ( ) = ( )

What's Left?

There are 4 toys all together.

Then, 1 toy falls.

How many are left?

$4 - 1 = \boxed{}$

Subtract to find each difference.

$9 - 1 = \boxed{}$ $\qquad$ $7 - 3 = \boxed{}$

$14 - 1 = \boxed{}$ $\qquad$ $8 - 3 = \boxed{}$

$18 - 4 = \boxed{}$ $\qquad$ $12 - 4 = \boxed{}$

$17 - 4 = \boxed{}$ $\qquad$ $16 - 4 = \boxed{}$

There are 5 toys all together.

1 toy leaves.

How many are left?

$5 - 1 =$ ⬚

Subtract to find each difference.

$18 - 2 =$ ⬚ $20 - 2 =$ ⬚

$18 - 3 =$ ⬚ $20 - 3 =$ ⬚

$18 - 4 =$ ⬚ $24 - 4 =$ ⬚

$18 - 5 =$ ⬚ $25 - 5 =$ ⬚

Learn Together

Make subtraction part of everyday activities. How many bananas are left when we eat 1 for breakfast? When we clean 4 dirty dishes, how many dirty dishes are left?

All Gone!

There are 25 fish on the reef.

How many are left when 10 fish leave?

You can solve 25 – 10 using a 50-chart.

Find 25 on the 50-chart. Jump back 10 to get 15.

1	2	3	4	5	6	7	8	9	10
11	12	13	14	15	16	17	18	19	20
21	22	23	24	25	26	27	28	29	30
31	32	33	34	35	36	37	38	39	40
41	42	43	44	45	46	47	48	49	50

Find each difference.

22 − 10 = ☐   23 − 10 = ☐

24 − 10 = ☐   26 − 10 = ☐

29 − 10 = ☐   38 − 20 = ☐

40 − 10 = ☐   43 − 10 = ☐

45 − 10 = ☐   50 − 10 = ☐

33 − 20 = ☐   38 − 20 = ☐

40 − 30 = ☐   44 − 30 = ☐

Learn Together

Discuss any patterns your child notices in some of their answers (subtracting 10 from a number means the first digit in the first two-digit number is one less than it was before). They can use those patterns to help them develop strategies for solving problems.

Take It Away!

Riley's emotions are helping her stay positive while she's completing math homework! You can help Riley with homework too by solving the subtraction sentences.

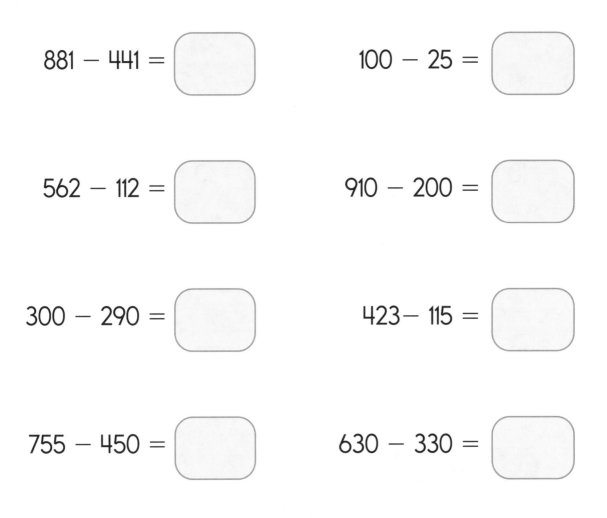

$881 - 441 =$

$100 - 25 =$

$562 - 112 =$

$910 - 200 =$

$300 - 290 =$

$423 - 115 =$

$755 - 450 =$

$630 - 330 =$

Solve these subtraction sentences.

238 − 128 = ☐   444 − 222 = ☐

560 − 330 = ☐   387 − 117 = ☐

900 − 400 = ☐   1,000 − 100 = ☐

819 − 110 = ☐   349 − 321 = ☐

746 − 116 = ☐   203 − 190 = ☐

Learn Together

With your child, create **subtraction stories** with numbers up to 1,000.

Less Cash

Look at the money.

Figure out how much money is left.

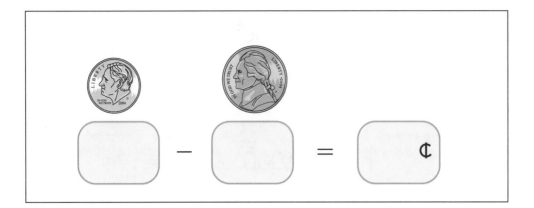

$$\boxed{} - \boxed{} = \boxed{} ¢$$

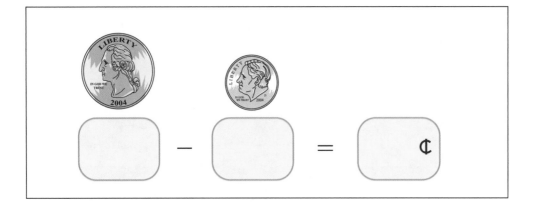

$$\boxed{} - \boxed{} = \boxed{} ¢$$

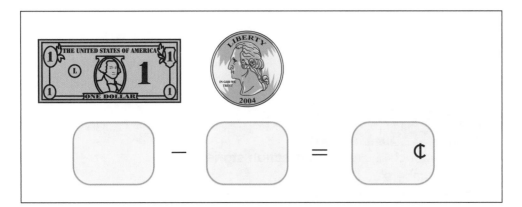

$$\boxed{} - \boxed{} = \boxed{} ¢$$

Look at the money.

Figure out how much money is left.

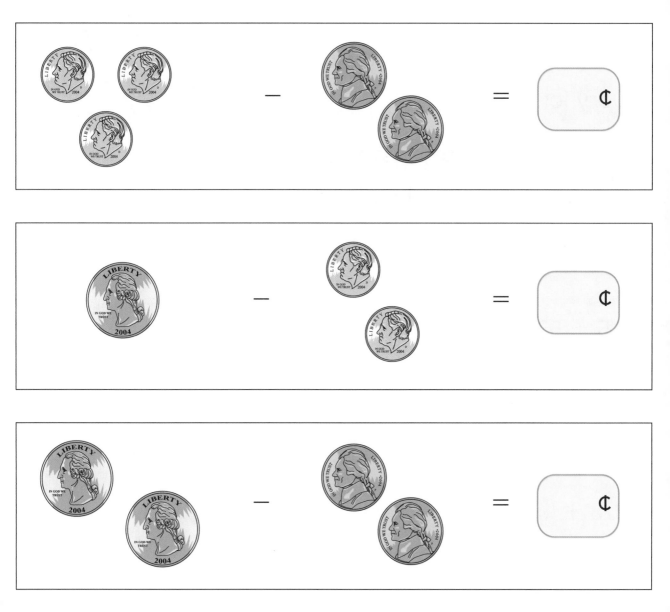

Learn Together

Help your child use real coins to make their calculations. Pose other subtraction problems for them to solve.

149

Adding Up and Taking Away

The otters are happy to have Dory for a friend!

Use the addition sentences to help you solve the related subtraction sentences.

$415 + 530 = 945$ $945 - 415 = \boxed{}$

$293 + 643 = 936$ $936 - 643 = \boxed{}$

$328 + 412 = 740$ $740 - 412 = \boxed{}$

$457 + 164 = 621$ $621 - 164 = \boxed{}$

Use the subtraction sentences to help you solve the related addition sentences.

719 + 182 = ☐   901 − 719 = 182

312 + 105 = ☐   417 − 105 = 312

591 + 120 = ☐   711 − 120 = 591

603 + 209 = ☐   812 − 209 = 603

252 + 130 = ☐   382 − 252 = 130

863 + 137 = ☐   1,000 − 863 = 137

912 + 78 = ☐   990 − 78 = 912

Learn Together

Help your child to see how each addition sentence is related to a subtraction sentence, and vice versa. Use blocks or toys to show the relationship for one set of sentences.

Some Super Humans

Dash is running late for school and needs quick homework help! Help him solve the addition and subtraction **word problems.**

Nasim and Miguel like to recycle. Nasim found and recycled 46 bottles. Miguel found and recycled 31 bottles.

How many bottles did they recycle in all?

$$46 + 31 = \boxed{}$$

Keep helping Dash solve the problems!

My school has a goal to plant 100 trees in one year. So far, we have planted 58.

How many more trees do we have to plant to reach our goal?

$$100 - 58 = \boxed{}$$

Jayden is trying to use less water when he showers. During his first shower he saves 15 gallons of water. During his second shower he saves 27 gallons of water.

How many gallons of water has he saved in all?

$$15 + 27 = \boxed{}$$

Learn Together

Help your child practice more addition and subtraction word problems about their everyday life. Ask them questions like, "If you ride your bike for 23 minutes today and 50 minutes tomorrow, how many minutes will you ride your bike in all?" Be sure the answers are within 100.

It Takes Two!

Some word problems ask you to solve two equations.

Solve the two-step word problems.
You might need addition and subtraction for some!

Dory is counting fish in the aquarium.

In one tank, she counts 10 purple fish.

In another tank, she counts 75 black fish.

In another tank, she counts 29 blue fish.

How many fish did Dory count in all?

Solve more two-step word problems.

Dory loves shells. She collected
23 shells on Monday, 67 shells on Tuesday, and
48 shells on Wednesday.

How many more shells did she collect on Monday
and Wednesday than on Tuesday?

There are 84 seals resting on the shore. First,
31 seals leave to hunt fish. Then, 52 more seals
leave to hunt fish.

How many seals are left on shore?

Learn Together

Help your child practice more two-step word problems about their everyday life. For example, you have to bake 60 cookies for the bake sale. If you bake 24 chocolate chip cookies and 28 peanut butter cookies, how many more cookies do you need to bake?

Odd or Even?

Edna Mode chooses masks for the Supers.

Groups of masks that can be separated evenly into pairs have an even number.

2   4

4 is an even number.

Groups that have one left over after they are paired have an odd number.

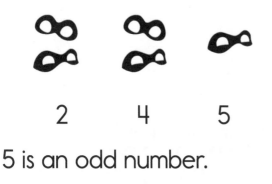

2   4   5

5 is an odd number.

Count and write the number for each group of masks. Then, label the groups odd or even.

_________ masks

____

_________ masks

____

_________ masks

____

Learn Together

Challenge your child to create other multiplication **arrays**. Encourage them to use 10-frames and counters to help them solve the problem.

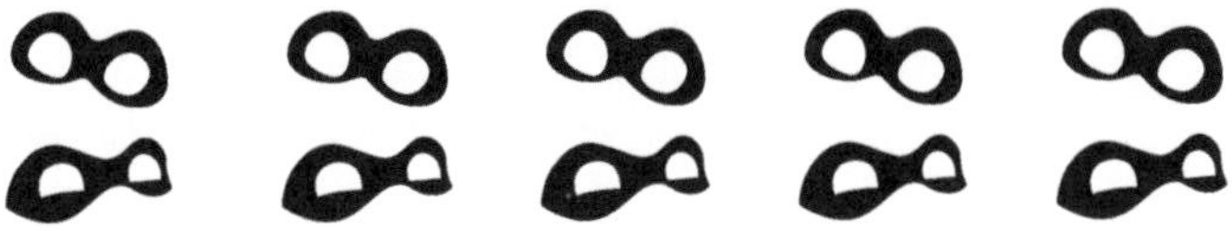

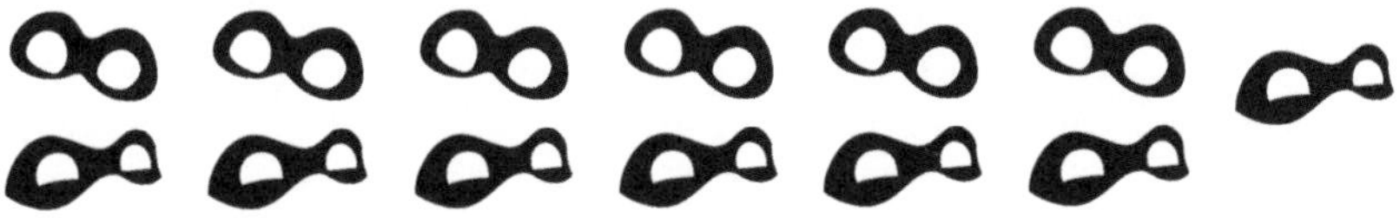

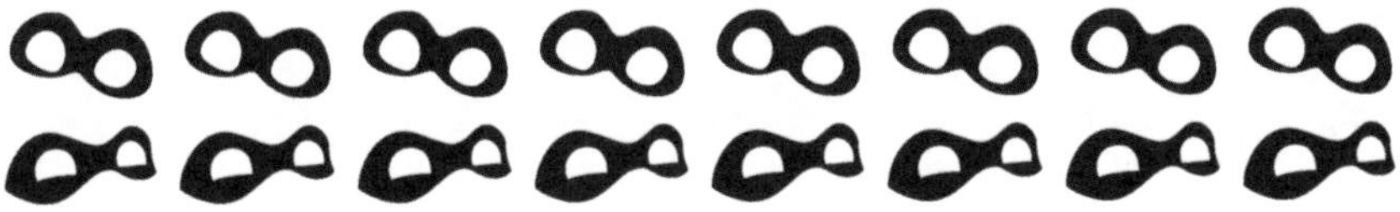

Joining Equal Groups

You multiply when you join equal groups.

Here are 4 groups of 2 fish.

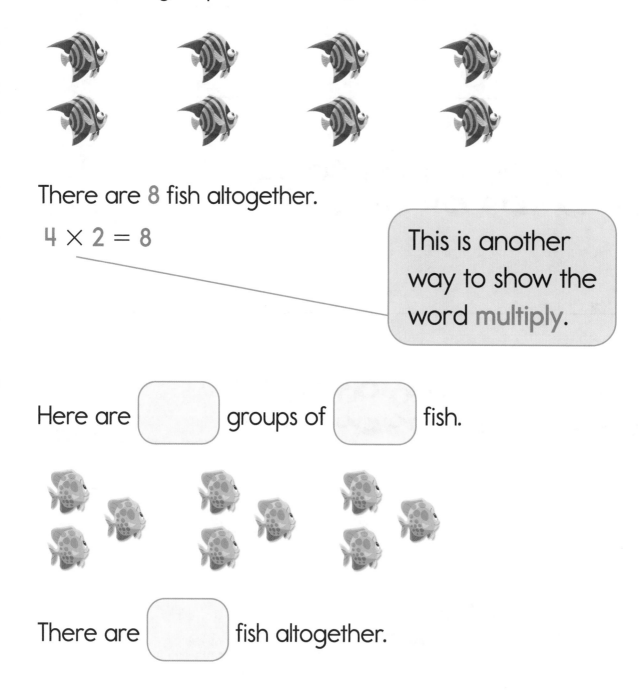

There are 8 fish altogether.

4 × 2 = 8

> This is another way to show the word multiply.

Here are ⬚ groups of ⬚ fish.

There are ⬚ fish altogether.

Here are [ ] groups of [ ] fish.

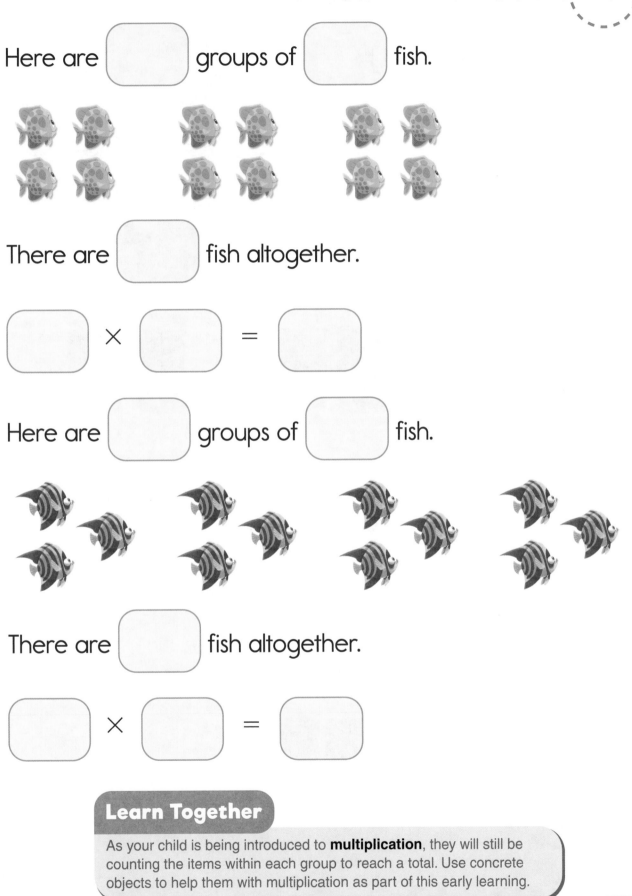

There are [ ] fish altogether.

[ ] × [ ] = [ ]

Here are [ ] groups of [ ] fish.

There are [ ] fish altogether.

[ ] × [ ] = [ ]

Learn Together

As your child is being introduced to **multiplication**, they will still be counting the items within each group to reach a total. Use concrete objects to help them with multiplication as part of this early learning.

Let's Multiply

Flo has many barrels of oil.

You can multiply to find out how many she has.

There are 3 groups of 2 barrels.

There are 6 barrels all together.

$3 \times 2 = 6$

There are 2 groups of 3 barrels.

$2 \times 3 = $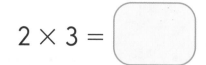

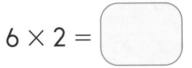

There are **6** groups of **2** barrels.

$6 \times 2 =$ ☐

There are **7** groups of **2** barrels.

$7 \times 2 =$ ☐

There are **3** groups of **3** barrels.

$3 \times 3 =$ ☐

Learn Together

Provide your child with other simple scenarios to practice multiplying. Say, "Let's multiply as we set the table. We need 3 sets of 4: 4 plates, 4 knives, and 4 forks. $3 \times 4 = 12$."

Separating Equal Groups

You **divide** when you want to share a group in equal parts.

1 race car has 4 tires.

How many race cars share **8** tires?

☐ race cars

How many race cars share **12** tires?

☐ race cars

How many race cars share 16 tires?

◻ race cars

How many race cars share 20 tires?

◻ race cars

How many race cars share 24 tires?

◻ race cars

Learn Together

Your child is just being introduced to the concept of **division**. Help your child solve these problems. Provide them with counters to arrange into groups of 4.

Mission Division

Sarge has 12 Green Army Men.

He needs to send them on 2 different missions.

He can divide them equally to find out how many to send on each mission.

This is another way to show the word divide.

$$12 \div 2 = 6$$

Circle groups of Green Army Men to show each division sentence

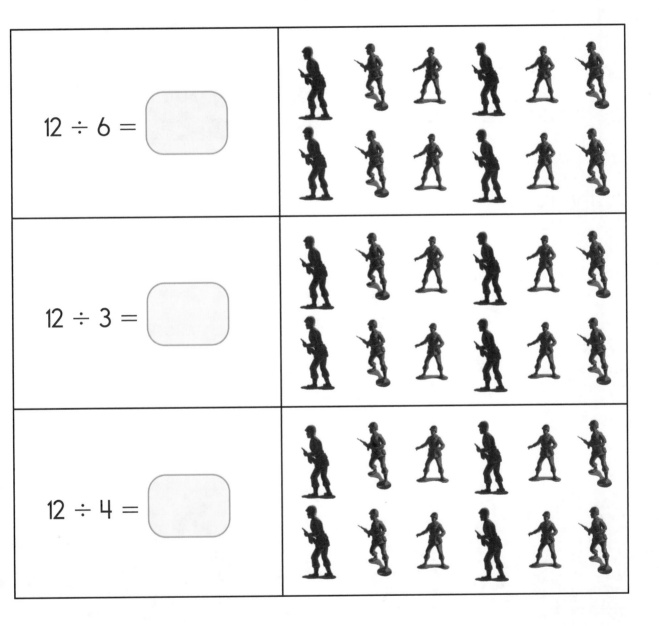

$12 \div 6 =$ ☐

$12 \div 3 =$ ☐

$12 \div 4 =$ ☐

Learn Together

Use objects like beads to find the answers and create other problems to solve. The idea of sharing is a familiar one for children, and can help them understand how one group might be divided into smaller equal groups.

Making Equal Groups

Show how the 10 fish below can be divided equally into 2 parts of the reef.

Each part of the reef has [ ] fish.

You have 20 marbles.

Fill each box with an equal number of marbles to show each division sentence.

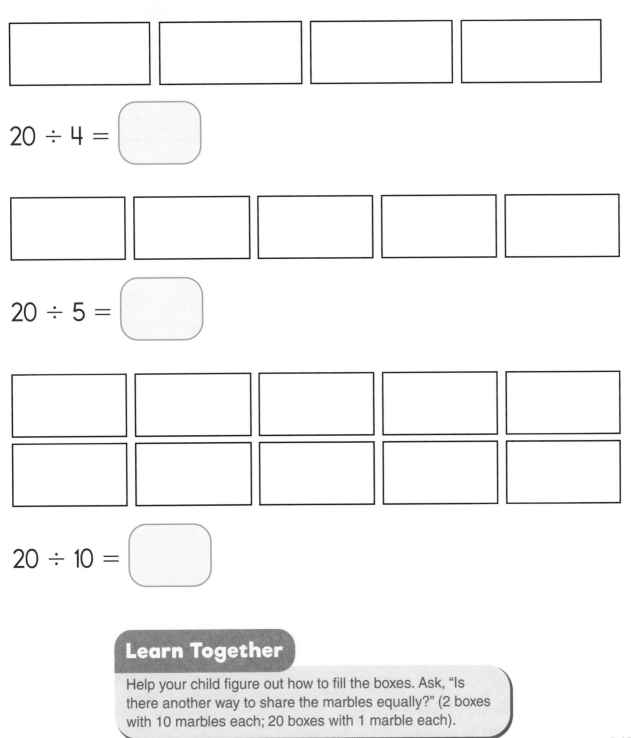

$20 \div 4 =$

$20 \div 5 =$

$20 \div 10 =$

Learn Together

Help your child figure out how to fill the boxes. Ask, "Is there another way to share the marbles equally?" (2 boxes with 10 marbles each; 20 boxes with 1 marble each).

Measure It!

Who is taller, Sadness or Joy?

You can measure people and objects to find out exactly how tall they are.

Use the ruler to measure the objects. You will use cenimeters (cm) and inches (in).

This domino is _____ cm long.

This crayon is _____ in. long.

Practice estimating how many feet.

My thumb is about _____ cm long.

My hand is about _____ in. long.

My arm is about _____ ft. long.

My foot is about _____ in. long.

My pencil is about _____ in. long.

My bed is about _____ ft. long.

My favorite toy is about _____ cm long.

Learn Together

If your child is using a ruler for the first time, they will need help to understand how to use it. They can measure other items using a ruler or tape measure. Discuss the terms *length*, *width*, and *height* and how they differ.

Incredibly Far

You can use feet to measure how far Elastigirl can stretch. A foot is a unit of measurement.

A foot is 12 inches long.

The symbol for feet is ft.

Draw something that is about 1 foot long.

Practice estimating how many feet.

How tall is a giraffe?

A giraffe is about _____ ft. tall.

How tall is a second grader?

A second grader is about _____ ft. tall.

How tall are you?

I am about _____ ft. tall.

Learn Together

Help your child measure their height.
Measure other objects using centimeters,
inches, feet, and meters.

Hold It!

Fillmore wants to know which containers hold about the **same**.

(Circle) the objects in each row that hold about the **same**.

Estimate how many glasses of water

each container will hold.

Circle the container that holds the **most**.

Container	Estimate	Actual Measurement
pitcher		
pot		
pan		

Learn Together

Provide your child with a glass and the other containers to help them estimate, and then measure how much each will hold. Find other containers around your home and create a chart like the one above.

Heavy or Light?

It's the Incredible family!

Who do you think
is the heaviest?

(Circle) the object in each pair that is heavier.

You can use a balance to compare the mass of two objects.

If you put two objects on a balance, how do you know which one is lighter?

_____

_____

_____

_____

_____

Learn Together

Help your child compare the mass of objects using a balance or a kitchen or bathroom scale. Note that your child may not yet have been introduced to units of measurement for mass.

How Big?

Estimate the number of squares that cover
this picture.

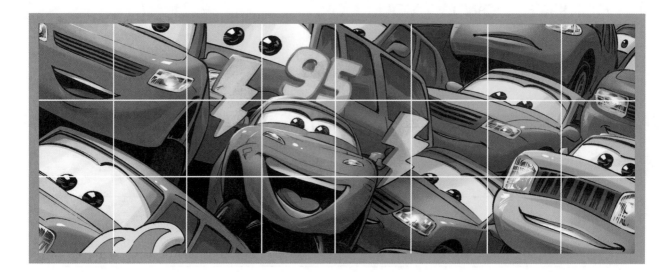

Now, count the number of squares that cover the
picture.

You figured out the **area** of the picture.

Area is the amount of space inside of a shape.

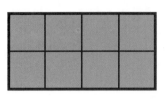

Estimate the area of this rectangle.

Count the squares.

The area is ⬜ squares.

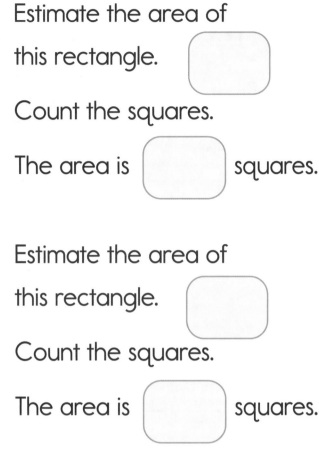

Estimate the area of this rectangle.

Count the squares.

The area is ⬜ squares.

Estimate the area of this rectangle.

Count the squares.

The area is ⬜ squares.

Learn Together

Work with your child to find the area of other objects. Use different items to cover the surface (cubes, blocks) and compare the area of each surface.

Counting the Days

Woody is interested in the calendar on Andy's wall.

Arrange these in order from shortest to longest.

month   week   year   day

How many months are in 1 year?

How many days are in 1 week?

Some months have 31 days.

Some months have 30 days.

February has 28 days, except every 4 years it has 29.

Put the month and numbers (or dates) on this calendar.

Month: _____

Sunday	Monday	Tuesday	Wednesday	Thursday	Friday	Saturday

Put a star on today's date.

How many days until the end of the month?

Learn Together

Help your child complete the calendar above for the current month. Plan activities using the calendar. Discuss how many days, or weeks, are left until certain events will occur.

Time Enough

It's time for Riley to go to bed.

Match each analog clock to the correct digital clock.

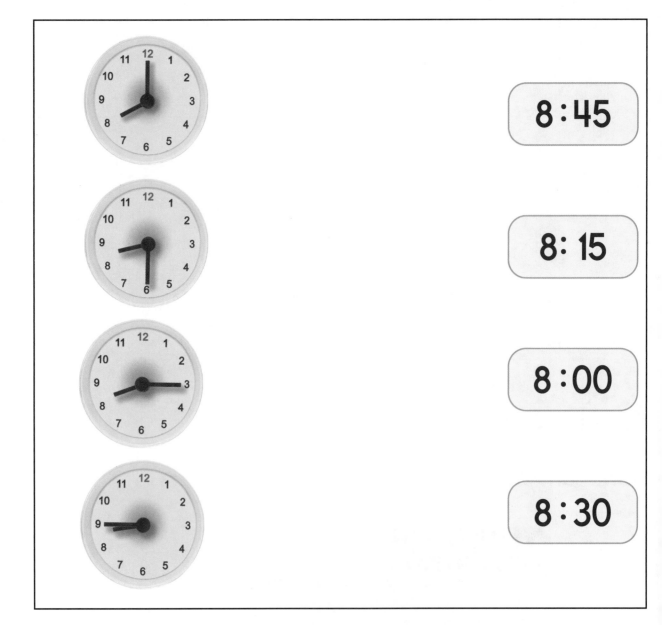

8 : 45

8 : 15

8 : 00

8 : 30

Show the time you wake up.

Show the time you eat lunch.

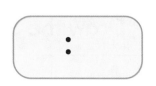

Show the time you go to bed.

© Disney/Pixar

Shaping Up

Hank can see many shapes when he escapes his tank.

What shapes do you see in this picture?

Complete the table below.

Shape	Draw the Shape	Number of Sides
square		
rectangle		
triangle		
circle		

Pentagons have 5 sides.

Trace this pentagon.

Now, draw your own pentagon.

Circle the pentagons.

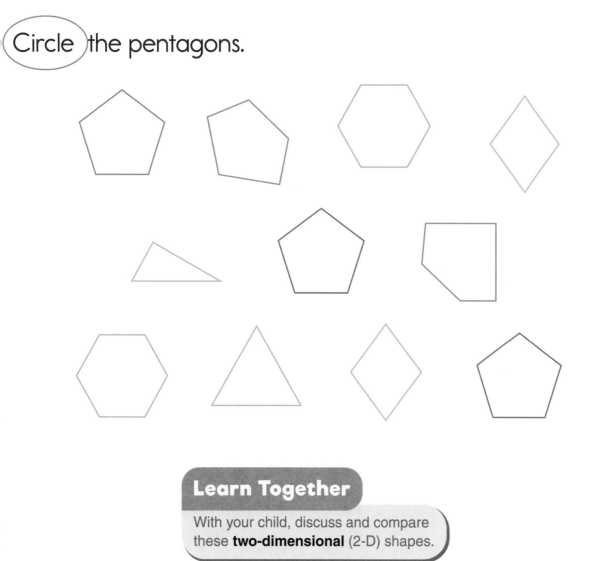

Learn Together

With your child, discuss and compare these **two-dimensional** (2-D) shapes.

Many Sides

Can you find a hexagon in this picture?

Hexagons have 6 sides.

Trace this hexagon.

Now, draw your own hexagon.

 the hexagons.

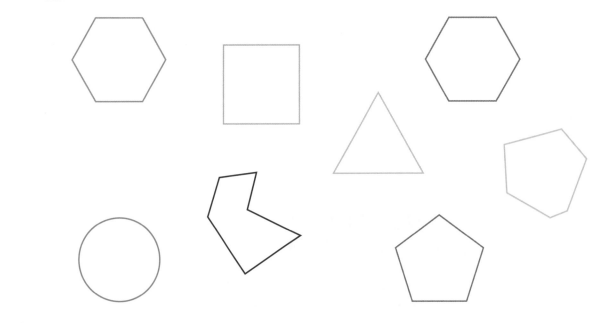

Octagons have **8** sides.

Trace this octagon.

Now, draw your own octagon.

Circle the octagons.

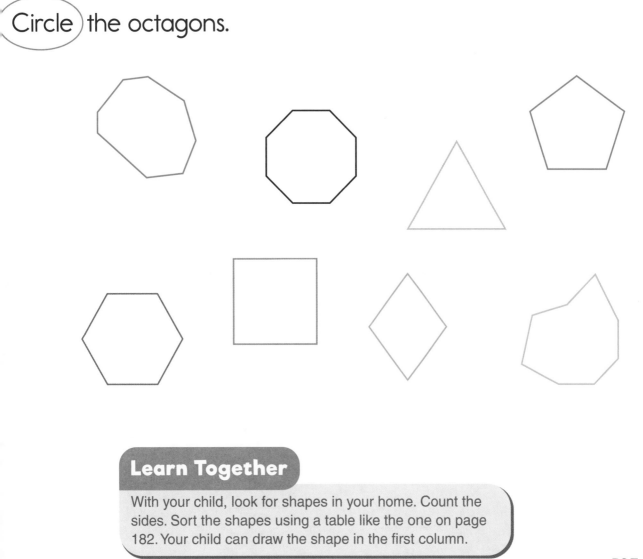

Learn Together

With your child, look for shapes in your home. Count the sides. Sort the shapes using a table like the one on page 182. Your child can draw the shape in the first column.

All Sorts of Shapes

Buzz is trapped in a carnival game! He is attached to a bunch of quadrilaterals. Quadrilaterals have 4 sides.

Squares, rectangles, and rhombuses are all quadrilaterals.

(Circle) the quadrilaterals.

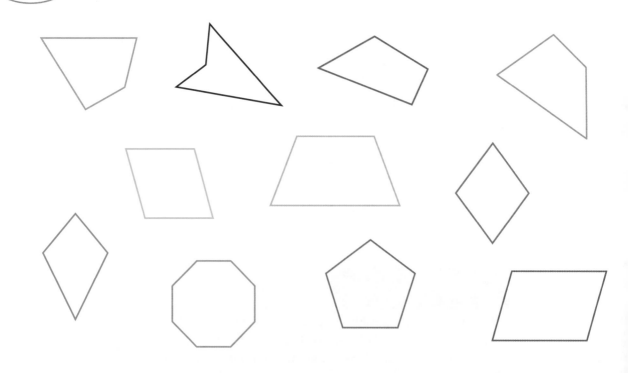

Complete the table below.

Shape	Draw the Shape	Number of Sides
pentagon		
hexagon		
octagon		
quadrilateral		

Shape Fun!

What shapes do you see in this truck?

What shapes make up the truck below? Label the shapes.

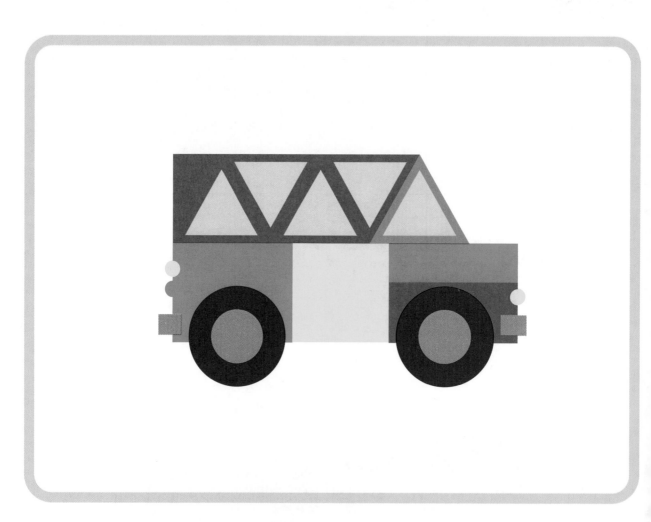

Use shapes to create your own truck!

Label your shapes.

Power Objects

Circle the 3-D objects you see in this picture.

Use these words to name each 3-D object below.

cube   cone   cylinder   sphere

_____

_____

_____

_____

Name one of the 3-D objects you circled in the picture.

_____

Use the clues to answer these riddles.

All my faces are the same and I have 8 vertices.

What am I? _____

I have one vertex and can roll.

What am I? _____

I have flat faces and can roll.

What am I? _____

I have no vertices and can roll.

What am I? _____

edge

vertex

face

Learn Together

Help your child create other riddles for **three-dimensional** (3-D) objects. Your child can create 3-D objects using modeling clay or other materials. They can describe and label the objects.

In 3-D

Can you find the cones
and spheres in this picture?

Cones and spheres are
3-D objects.

Pyramids and prisms are also 3-D objects.

Use these words to name each 3-D object below.

triangular prism   square pyramid
rectangular prism

 _____

 _____

 _____

Use the clues to
answer these riddles.

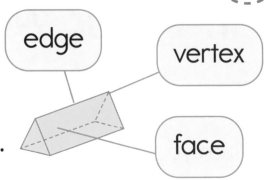

edge

vertex

face

I have six faces and can stack.

What am I? _____

I have five faces and five vertices.

What am I? _____

I have two triangular faces and three rectangular
faces.

What am I? _____

Write another riddle for one 3-D object.

_____

Learn Together

Talk about how some shapes can roll and some shapes can stack
(and some can do both). Use blocks or other objects to experiment
to find out which 3-D objects are best for stacking and rolling.

Find Your Way

Dory needs to find her parents.

When you need to find something, you might use a map.

Examine the map below.

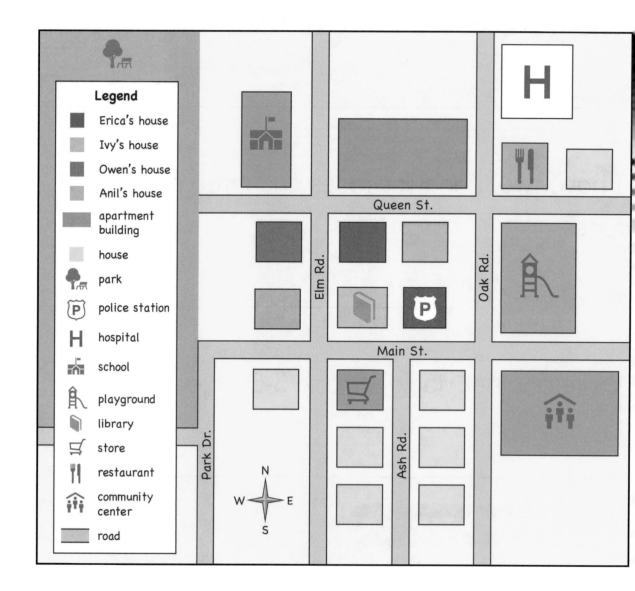

Start at Erica's house.

Walk east along Queen Street.

Turn north on Oak Road. Walk to the end of the street.

Where are you? _____

Write directions from the hospital to the store.

_____

_____

_____

Write directions from the community center to the library.

_____

_____

Learn Together

Examine the map together. Help your child create a map of your neighborhood. As you work, use phrases such as *behind*, *near, far,* and *in front of* to describe location. Use the map to create directions for another person to follow.

What Are the Chances?

Jackson Storm

Chuck Armstrong

Lightning McQueen

Manny Flywheel

Cruz Ramirez

Look at the picture.

Circle the word that best describes each statement.

Lightning McQueen will win the race.

likely   unlikely   certain   impossible

Chuck Armstrong will win the race.

likely   unlikely   certain   impossible

Manny Flywheel will win the race.

likely   unlikely   certain   impossible

Chuck Armstrong will finish the race before
Jackson Storm.

likely   unlikely   certain   impossible

This race will have a winner.

likely   unlikely   certain   impossible

Write your own **probability** statement
about the race.

_____

_____

Learn Together

Discuss the meaning of each probability phrase with your
child. Encourage them to use one of these phrases as
they write a new statement. Play games with spinners or
dice to help your child learn about probability.

© Disney/Pixar

197

Picturing Numbers

A bar graph uses bars to show data.

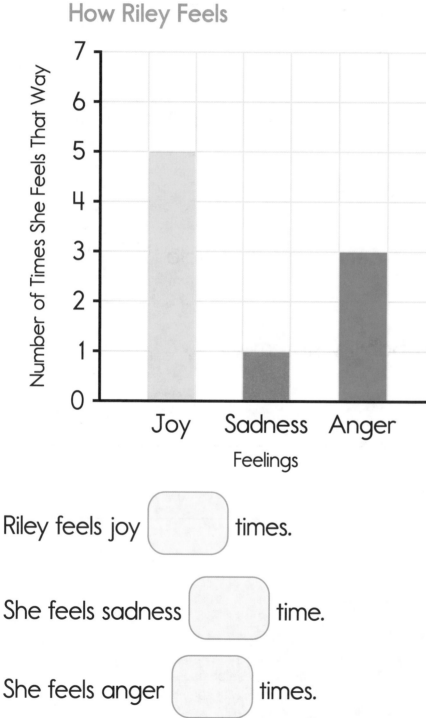

How Riley Feels

Riley feels joy ☐ times.

She feels sadness ☐ time.

She feels anger ☐ times.

Create a bar graph to show
how you felt yesterday.

I felt joy _____ times.

I felt sadness _____ times.

I felt anger _____ times.

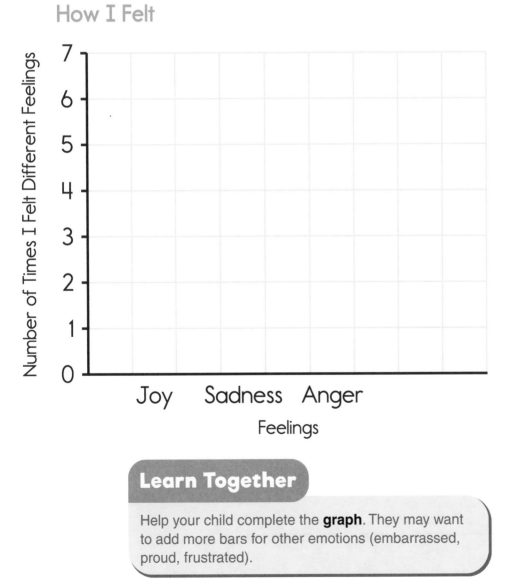

How I Felt

Number of Times I Felt Different Feelings (y-axis: 0, 1, 2, 3, 4, 5, 6, 7)

Joy   Sadness   Anger

Feelings

Graph Up

Woody asks his friends what color he should color with.

Their color choices are on this line plot.

A line plot uses an x to show how many times something happened.

Color Choices

How many friends want the color

to be blue? _____

Create a line plot.

Show the favorite ice cream flavors

of your family or friends.

Favorite Ice Cream Flavors

Vanilla   Chocolate   Strawberry

Flavors

What does your line plot tell you?

_____

_____

Learn Together

Help your child create other line plots. Ask them
questions about the most and least popular choices.

Language Arts

As your child completes the lessons in this book, extend their learning with some of the following activities.

Letter Recognition

- Help your child arrange objects in alphabetical order.

- Together, sort books into alphabetical order on your child's bookshelf. Decide whether it will be alphabetical by title or author's last name.

- At the store, encourage your child to look at how the spices are organized (usually in alphabetical order). Name a spice for them to find. Take turns finding spices you each name.

- Your child is surrounded by environmental print. Examples include signs, labels, maps, and advertising. Encourage them to read environmental print, praising their growing reading ability.

Phonics

- Your child can highlight word patterns they see (such as the long o sound in road, boat, soap; adding -ed to some verbs to make the past tense). They can begin a word knowledge notebook for word patterns and word families.

- As your child's reading skills develop, they will notice many exceptions to general rules (the ei in eight makes a long a sound, not a long e sound; past tense of swim is swam, not swimmed). Challenge them to add these rules and exceptions to their word knowledge notebook.

- Use fridge magnets or flash cards to create word families (short vowel: -ad, -at, -et, -ed; long vowel: -ape, -aid, -eet, -eed). Your child can experiment with adding consonants to make words (dad, pad, mad, sad; deed, seed, feed).

Word Knowledge

- Create a three-column chart for nouns—person, place, thing. Give your child a minute to list as many nouns as they can think of.

- Together, play a game of charades. Take turns acting out a verb. Use the following hand signals to show verb tense:
  - Thumb pointing backward = past
  - Finger pointing down = present tense
  - Finger pointing forward = future tense

Comprehension

- As you read books or watch shows, ask your child questions to help them make predictions and inferences. ("Riley is unhappy about moving. What do you think she's going to do?")

- Encourage your child's questions about stories and nonfiction text.

- Use wordless picture books to help your child practice making inferences and drawing conclusions.

- To practice making inferences, play Paper Bag Mysteries. Add some clues about a familiar character to a paper bag. Your child can remove the clues one by one and start to make inferences about who the character is.

- The classic game of Twenty Questions requires your child to make inferences.

- As you read the title of a book, ask: "What do you think the story is about? Who is the main character? Do you think the story will be happy, sad, or something else? Why?"

- Your child will still need support identifying the main idea. As you watch movies together, discuss the main idea. Challenge them to summarize the movie.

- Pictures help your child make sense of text. Encourage your child to examine the pictures closely to understand what has happened, where a story is set, or how characters are feeling.

Writing

- Create a mystery message together for someone else to read—omit the first letter of each word.

- Create sentence starters for your child to finish. ("I want a _____. Do you want to go to the _____? I love _____.")

- Create a digital photo album together, with photos of your child's life. They can write simple captions.

- With your child, write stories, lists, letters, poems, and other texts.

- Write notes to one another and leave them in secret places.

- Together, create a treasure map for your child to follow.

- Your child can write labels or captions for their drawings.

- As your child writes using various verb tenses, encourage them to say the sentence to figure out form and spelling. Look for patterns that can help them (ending some verbs with -ed) and for exceptions to rules (ate/eat; got/get; went/go) that they can add to their word knowledge notebook.

- What kind of superheroes would you and your child like to be? Draw pictures of yourselves as superheroes. Label the parts of your costumes and write captions for your pictures.

Math

Number Sense

- Using 100 small objects, make number groups (40 objects, 60 objects). Your child can write the number and the word for that number. Make up word problems using the objects.

- Create 10-frame boxes to help your child count objects. Create a hundreds chart and provide your child with 100 counters (buttons, beads) to cover it to help them with addition and subtraction.

- Invite your child to help you cook and bake. Point out how many recipes use fractions. Can they figure out how much of each ingredient is needed?

- Count backward from 100 together, pausing now and then to let your child fill in the number.

Patterns

- Encourage your child to sort objects, such as toys, by providing them with bins or other containers. Talk about the rules they are using to sort. ("All of the red toys went in the red bin. Are you sorting by color?")

- Your child can sort their laundry as they put it away. What rule will they use?

- Mix some objects into a bin (pens, toys, spoons). What rule will your child use to sort the objects?

- As you take out or put away seasonal decorations, allow your child to help sort the objects (by color, purpose, material, size, and so on).

- Look for patterns in nature and around your home.

- Give your child objects to create patterns with (blocks, buttons, school supplies, toys).

- Create a pattern and ask your child to add to it. Ask your child to create a pattern for you to finish.

Addition and Subtraction

- With your child, create a number line from zero to 100. Give them groups of objects to add and subtract.

- Play games involving skip counting ("hide and seek" with the searcher counting to 100 by 5s). Skip count by 2s, 5s, 10s, and 100s together.

- Use connecting blocks to make counting cubes (1s, 10s, and 100s) for solving problems. ("If I have two hundreds blocks, two tens blocks, and three ones blocks, how many blocks do I have altogether?").

Multiplication and Division

- Look for natural sets in your home that can be used for problems involving multiplication and division (two cases of juice boxes; 12 cans of soup).

- When you shop, provide opportunities to multiply and divide. Say, "If we need three apples a day for five days, how many apples do we need? This pizza has 12 pieces, and 4 people will eat it. How many pieces does each person get?"

Measurement

- Encourage your child to compare the length, width, or height of various items. Ask: "Is your glass taller than a pencil? Is your book wider than a favorite toy?"

- Use your cellphone to look for geocaches in your neighborhood. Your child will enjoy the adventure of finding hidden objects as they learn how to follow directions and navigate.

- With your child, talk about the timing of events. "Next Wednesday, we'll go swimming at seven o'clock. But that means we'll need to eat half an hour earlier. What time should we eat?"

Geometry

- Look for 3-D objects in your home, noting their shapes (cans are cylinders). Your child can draw and label the objects and shapes.

- Look for shapes as you take a walk in your neighborhood. ("That door is a rectangle. The window is a square.")

- Look for 3-D objects in your neighborhood. If possible, let your child examine and touch all the sides.

- Look for maps as you are out with your child—in shopping malls, parks, and bus stations. Examine the maps together.

- Use position words to describe the location of places.

Collecting and Using Data

- Play games that include an element of probability (any game that includes dice, spinners, or cards).

- Discuss the outcome of events using words such as *unlikely*, *certain*, and *impossible*.

- Look for graphs and tables as you read nonfiction texts together. Ask questions about the graphs and tables.

Glossary

100-chart: a table that displays the numbers from 1 to 100 (or 0 to 99). This chart can be a useful tool for your child when skip counting, adding, or subtracting.

10-frames: two-by-five rectangle frames used to help teach counting. Counters are placed to illustrate numbers less than or equal to ten.

addition sentence: a number sentence or equation used to express addition (4 + 1 = 5).

adjective: a word that describes a noun. Lightning McQueen is **fast**.

adverb: a word that describes a verb. Adverbs will often answer questions when, where, or how? Cruz races **skillfully**.

alphabetical order: arrangement according to the order of letters in the alphabet.

antonyms: words that mean the opposite of another word. Mater is **slow,** but Lightning McQueen is **fast**.

area: the number of unit squares that can cover a flat surface.

arrays: arrangements of items in rows or columns to make it easier to count or calculate totals.

chart: (or table) a graphic organizer used to sort and organize information in ways that make it easier to read, compare it, and understand it.

collective noun: a word that names a group of people or things. Some collective nouns include **fleet** (of ships) **flock** (of birds) and **litter** (of kittens).

common nouns: nouns that name general people, places, or things. Some common nouns are **dogs**, **tree**, **girl**, **park**.

compound word: a word composed of two or more smaller words (**background**). Your child can sometimes use their knowledge of the smaller words to figure out the meaning of the compound word.

consonant blends: two or more consonants that work together in a word, where each consonant can be distinctly heard (the **sn** in **snake** or the **ft** in **raft**).

context: the words or text surrounding an unfamiliar word that can be used to help clarify the meaning of that word.

contractions: words created by joining two words using an apostrophe to replace the missing letters (**don't, I'm, you're**).

digraphs: two letters working together in a word to make one sound (the **sh** in **shake** or the **ck** in **block**).

division: the math operation that splits into equal groups.

draw conclusions: to make decisions about or evaluations of the events or characters in stories. This reading strategy supports your child's understanding of texts, but also requires them to apply critical thinking skills that are still developing.

estimating: to use your understanding of numbers to make an educated guess at an answer to a problem.

fact: true information that can be proven or supported. To become a critical reader and thinker, your child will need to differentiate between facts and opinions.

homophones: words that sound the same but are spelled differently (**to/two/too**). It is natural when your child writes for them to still be spelling homophones incorrectly.

graph: a diagram that shows the relationship between data points.

irregular verbs: verbs that do not follow the standard tense endings (**is/was**).

make inferences: to use clues in the text to "read between the lines." This reading strategy requires your child to use their critical thinking skills as well as their background knowledge and understanding of texts.

make predictions: to form an educated guess about what will happen next. This strategy supports your child's understanding of texts.

making connections: a reading strategy that requires your child to use their background knowledge; this strategy supports your child's understanding of texts. There are three types of connections (text to self, text to text, and text to world).

multiplication: the math operation that adds a number to itself a number of times; repeated addition.

number line: a line showing numbers along it, placed in order. Number lines can help your child as they add, subtract, or think about how one number is related to another (3 comes before 6, 10 is 9 numbers away from 1).

opinion: a personal statement or belief. For example, blue is the best color.

phonics: the sounds letters or groups of letters make.

place value: the value a number holds based on its position within a larger number. For example, in the number 324 there are 3 hundreds, 2 tens, and 4 ones. So, 3 is in the hundreds place, 2 is in the tens place, and 4 is in the ones place.

plural words: words that indicate there is more than one of something. There are rules, and exceptions to those rules, to follow when making a word plural (baby/babies; child/children; person/people). Your child is just learning these rules as they spell, but will probably already be following the rules when speaking.

prefixes: letters added to the beginning of a word to change the meaning (**re**turn, **un**done).

probability: the chance or likelihood of something happening. Help your child predict the outcome of events (ranging from impossible to certain) as an introduction to this math concept.

proper nouns: nouns that name a specific person, place, or thing; they are capitalized, even if they're not at the start of a sentence.

silent letters: letters in a word you do not hear when spoken (**k** in **knife**, **b** in **comb**). Your child is at a stage when they will spell many words as they sound, and not add the silent letters. Encourage them to think about word patterns or families, where appropriate (**know**, **knowledge**; **when**, **where**, **what**) or to make up memory aids to remember the spelling ("B sure to comb your hair every day.").

skip counting: to count in increments other than one (2, 4, 6, 8, 10). Your child will be skip counting by 2s, 5s, 10s, and hundreds.

story elements: characters, setting, and plot are the features of a story. When your child can identify story elements, they develop their understanding and appreciation of the story.

subtraction sentence: a number sentence or equation used to express subtraction (4 − 1 + 3).

subtraction stories: one or more statements that illustrate a math subtraction equation. For example, the equation 4 − 2 = 2 could be told as a story about four children who are playing, but two friends leave.

suffix: letters added to the end of a word to change its meaning (small**er**).

synonyms: words that have the same or almost the same meaning. Dory is **happy** and **cheerful**.

three-dimensional: Something that has length, width, and depth. Shapes that are three-dimensional include spheres, cubes, and pyramids.

two-dimensional: having length and width but no depth. Shapes that are two-dimensional include circles, squares, and triangles.

verb tenses: the varying form of the verb that expresses a time frame—past, present, or future.

verbs: action words; note that the spelling rules for verbs can be complex, particularly irregular verbs, which take unusual forms depending on how they are used with other words or in other tenses (eat/ate, am/are/is—for to be, go/went, swim/swam).

word ending: the letters at the end of a word that form a sound or make the word part of a word family. Your child is using common word endings to help them read new words (fight/right/might; flow/blow/know); knowing how one of these words is pronounced helps them know how to pronounce other words with the same ending.

word family: a group of words related in some way. For example, they begin or end with the same sound (bed, fed, red are part of the -ed word family; black, blue, blond are part of the bl word family).

word problems: math problems that use real-life situations and objects to represent an equation.

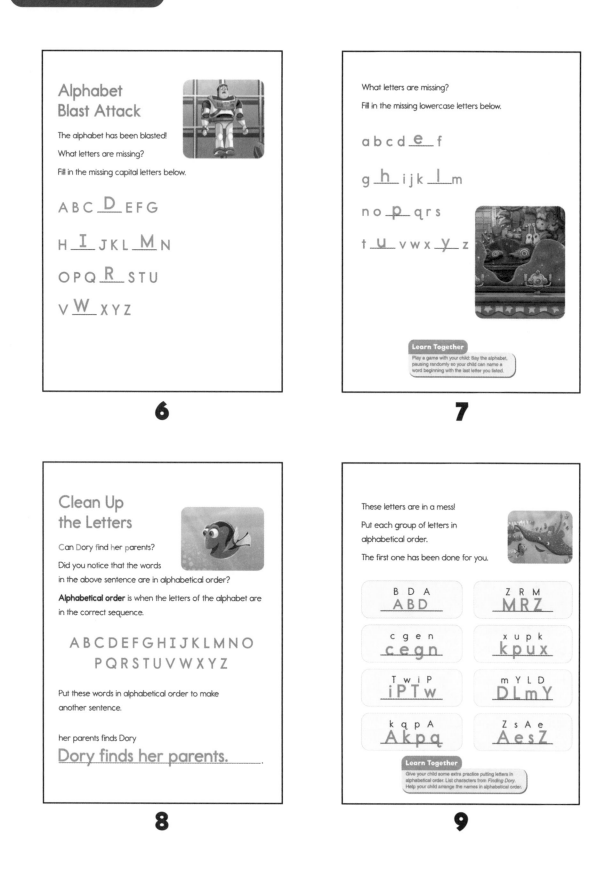

Alphabet Blast Attack

The alphabet has been blasted!

What letters are missing?

Fill in the missing capital letters below.

A B C **D** E F G

H **I** J K L **M** N

O P Q **R** S T U

V **W** X Y Z

6

What letters are missing?

Fill in the missing lowercase letters below.

a b c d **e** f

g **h** i j k **l** m

n o **p** q r s

t **u** v w x **y** z

Learn Together

Play a game with your child: Say the alphabet, pausing randomly so your child can name a word beginning with the last letter you listed.

7

Clean Up the Letters

Can Dory find her parents?

Did you notice that the words in the above sentence are in alphabetical order?

Alphabetical order is when the letters of the alphabet are in the correct sequence.

A B C D E F G H I J K L M N O
P Q R S T U V W X Y Z

Put these words in alphabetical order to make another sentence.

her parents finds Dory

Dory finds her parents.

8

These letters are in a mess!

Put each group of letters in alphabetical order.

The first one has been done for you.

B D A
A B D

Z R M
M R Z

c g e n
c e g n

x u p k
k p u x

T w i P
i P T w

m Y L D
D L m Y

k q p A
A k p q

Z s A e
A e s Z

Learn Together

Give your child some extra practice putting letters in alphabetical order. List characters from *Finding Dory*. Help your child arrange the names in alphabetical order.

9

Alphabet Rescue!

A family saves the world.

Did you notice that the words in the above sentence are in alphabetical order?

Put these words in alphabetical order.

fast   strong   incredible

fast incredible strong

robot   hero   save

hero robot save

team   super   mask

mask super team

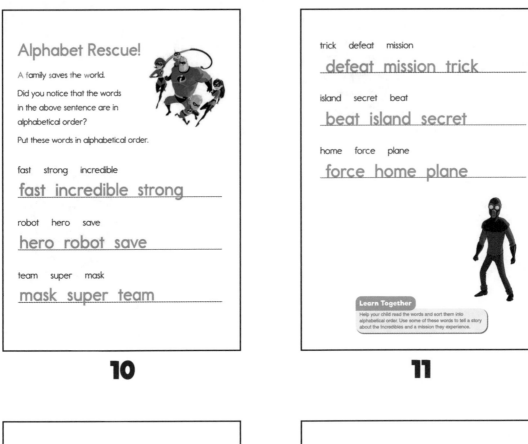

10

---

trick   defeat   mission

defeat mission trick

island   secret   beat

beat island secret

home   force   plane

force home plane

Learn Together

Help your child read the words and sort them into alphabetical order. Use some of these words to tell a story about the Incredibles and a mission they experience.

11

Missing Letters

Can you figure out which letter is missing?

rainbow   **h**elp

lobster   **m**other   l   h   m   r

Read each word out loud.

Listen to the sound of the first letter.

12

Add the missing letters.

h   l   r   m

Dory **L**oses **h**er way.

How will she find the **r**ight way to go?

Lost Dory **m**isses **h**er **m**om and dad.

Read each sentence out loud.

Listen to the letter sounds.

Write your own sentence about Dory.

Dory loves her mom and dad.

Answers will vary.

Learn Together

Help your child figure out which letter goes at the beginning of each word. Using **phonics** skills, they can try each of the letters, then sound out the word to see if it makes sense in the word or the sentence.

13

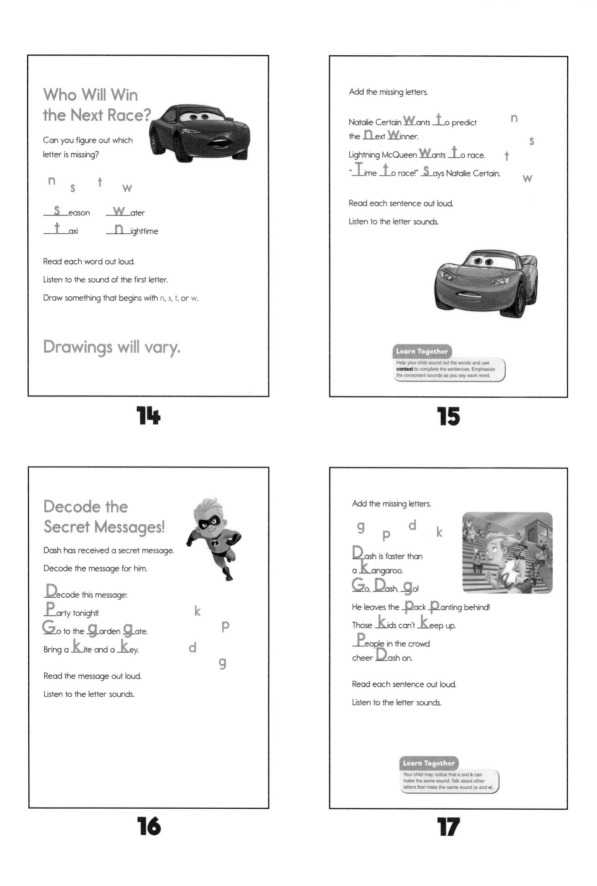

Who Will Win the Next Race?

Can you figure out which letter is missing?

n s t w

__S__eason __W__ater

__t__axi __n__ightime

Read each word out loud.

Listen to the sound of the first letter.

Draw something that begins with n, s, t, or w.

Drawings will vary.

14

Add the missing letters.

n s t w

Natalie Certain __W__ants __t__o predict the __n__ext __W__inner.

Lightning McQueen __W__ants __t__o race.

"__T__ime __t__o race!" __S__ays Natalie Certain.

Read each sentence out loud.

Listen to the letter sounds.

Learn Together
Help your child sound out the words and use **context** to complete the sentences. Emphasize the consonant sounds as you say each word.

15

Decode the Secret Messages!

Dash has received a secret message.

Decode the message for him.

__D__ecode this message:

__P__arty tonight!

__G__o to the __g__arden __g__ate.

Bring a __k__ite and a __k__ey.

k p d g

Read the message out loud.

Listen to the letter sounds.

16

Add the missing letters.

g p d k

__D__ash is faster than a __k__angaroo.

__G__o, __D__ash, __g__o!

He leaves the __p__ack __p__anting behind!

Those __k__ids can't __k__eep up.

__P__eople in the crowd cheer __D__ash on.

Read each sentence out loud.

Listen to the letter sounds.

Learn Together
Your child may notice that c and k can make the same sound. Talk about other letters that make the same sound (c and s).

17

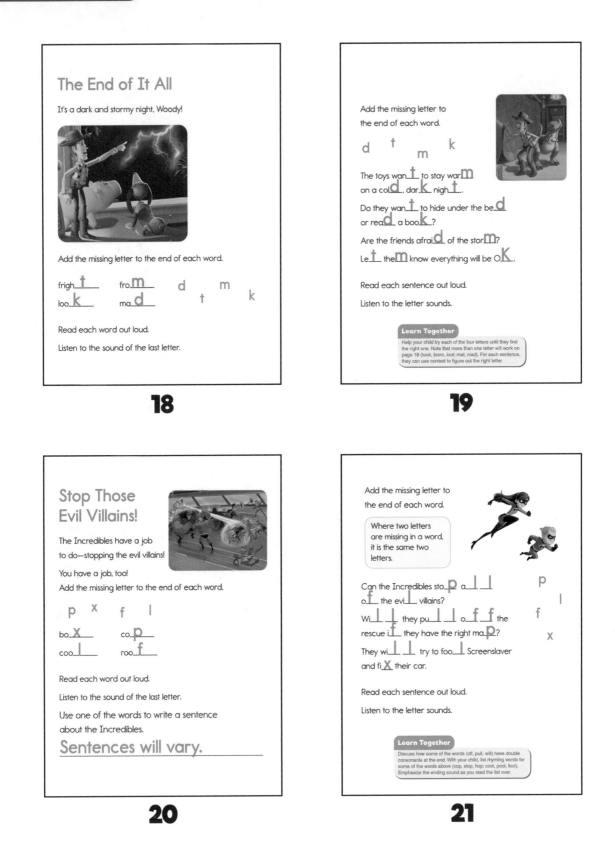

The End of It All

It's a dark and stormy night, Woody!

Add the missing letter to the end of each word.

frigh**t**   fro**m**   d   t   m   k
loo**k**   ma**d**   t   k

Read each word out loud.

Listen to the sound of the last letter.

18

Add the missing letter to
the end of each word.

d   t   m   k

The toys wan**t** to stay war**m**
on a col**d**, dar**k** nigh**t**.
Do they wan**t** to hide under the be**d**
or rea**d** a boo**k**?
Are the friends afrai**d** of the stor**m**?
Le**t** the**m** know everything will be O**K**.

Read each sentence out loud.

Listen to the letter sounds.

Learn Together
Help your child try each of the four letters until they find
the right one. Note that more than one letter will work on
page 18 (look, loom, loot; mat, mad). For each sentence,
they can use context to figure out the right letter.

19

Stop Those Evil Villains!

The Incredibles have a job
to do--stopping the evil villains!

You have a job, too!
Add the missing letter to the end of each word.

p   x   f   l

bo**x**   co**p**
coo**l**   roo**f**

Read each word out loud.

Listen to the sound of the last letter.

Use one of the words to write a sentence
about the Incredibles.

Sentences will vary.

20

Add the missing letter to
the end of each word.

Where two letters
are missing in a word,
it is the same two
letters.

Can the Incredibles sto**p** a**ll**   p
o**ff** the evi**l** villains?
Wi**ll** they pu**ll** o**ff** the   f
rescue i**f** they have the right ma**p**?   x
They wi**ll** try to foo**l** Screenslaver
and fi**x** their car.

Read each sentence out loud.

Listen to the letter sounds.

Learn Together
Discuss how some of the words (off, pull, will) have double
consonants at the end. With your child, list rhyming words for
some of the words above (cop, stop, hop; cool, pool, tool).
Emphasize the ending sound as you read the list over.

21

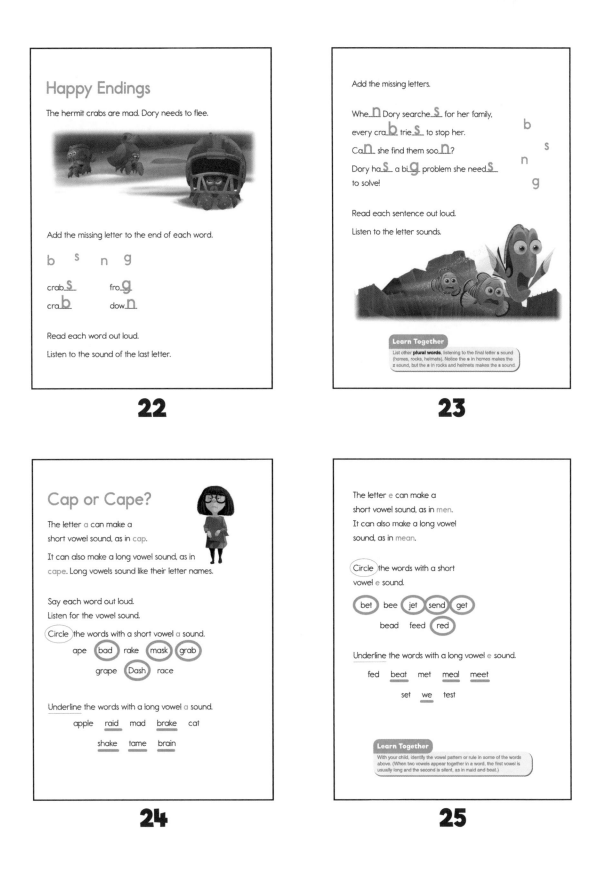

Happy Endings

The hermit crabs are mad. Dory needs to flee.

Add the missing letter to the end of each word.

b   s   n   g

crab**s**   fro**g**
cra**b**   dow**n**

Read each word out loud.

Listen to the sound of the last letter.

22

Add the missing letters.

Whe**n** Dory searche**s** for her family,
every cra**b** trie**s** to stop her.
Ca**n** she find them soo**n**?
Dory ha**s** a bi**g** problem she need**s**
to solve!

b
s
n
g

Read each sentence out loud.

Listen to the letter sounds.

Learn Together
List other **plural words**, listening to the final letter s sound
(homes, rocks, helmets). Notice the s in homes makes the
z sound, but the s in rocks and helmets makes the s sound.

23

Cap or Cape?

The letter a can make a
short vowel sound, as in cap.

It can also make a long vowel sound, as in
cape. Long vowels sound like their letter names.

Say each word out loud.
Listen for the vowel sound.

Circle the words with a short vowel a sound.

ape (bad) rake (mask) (grab)

grape (Dash) race

Underline the words with a long vowel a sound.

apple raid mad brake cat

shake tame brain

24

The letter e can make a
short vowel sound, as in men.
It can also make a long vowel
sound, as in mean.

Circle the words with a short
vowel e sound.

(bet) bee (jet) (send) (get)

bead feed (red)

Underline the words with a long vowel e sound.

fed beat met meal meet

set we test

Learn Together
With your child, identify the vowel pattern or rule in some of the words
above. (When two vowels appear together in a word, the first vowel is
usually long and the second is silent, as in maid and beat.)

25

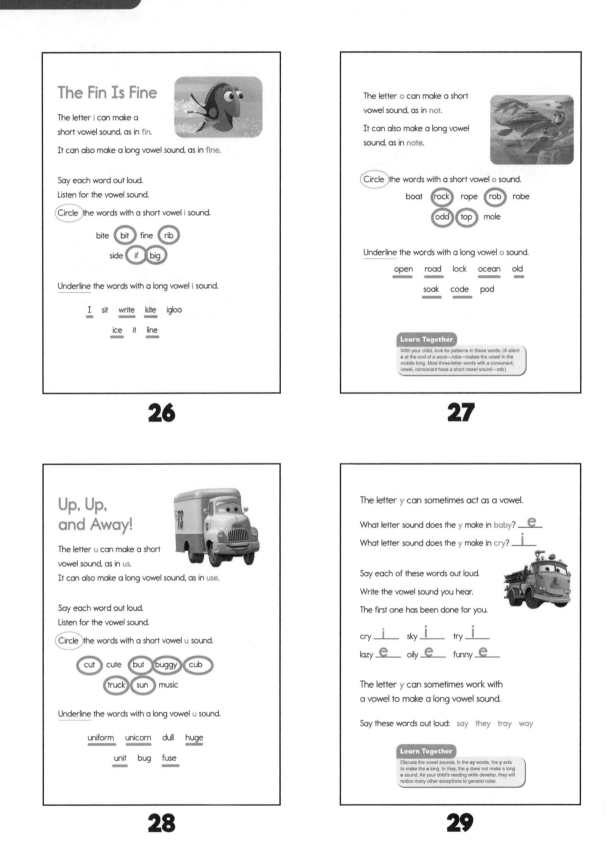

The Fin Is Fine

The letter i can make a
short vowel sound, as in fin.

It can also make a long vowel sound, as in fine.

Say each word out loud.
Listen for the vowel sound.

Circle the words with a short vowel i sound.

bite (bit) fine (rib)
side (if) (big)

Underline the words with a long vowel i sound.

I̱ sit write kite igloo

ice it line

26

The letter o can make a short
vowel sound, as in not.

It can also make a long vowel
sound, as in note.

Circle the words with a short vowel o sound.

boat (rock) rope (rob) robe

(odd) (top) mole

Underline the words with a long vowel o sound.

open road lock ocean old

soak code pod

Learn Together
With your child, look for patterns in these words. (A silent
e at the end of a word—robe—makes the vowel in the
middle long. Most three-letter words with a consonant,
vowel, consonant have a short vowel sound—rob.)

27

Up, Up, and Away!

The letter u can make a short
vowel sound, as in us.
It can also make a long vowel sound, as in use.

Say each word out loud.
Listen for the vowel sound.

Circle the words with a short vowel u sound.

(cut) cute (but) (buggy) (cub)

(truck) (sun) music

Underline the words with a long vowel u sound.

uniform unicorn dull huge

unit bug fuse

28

The letter y can sometimes act as a vowel.

What letter sound does the y make in baby? __e__
What letter sound does the y make in cry? __i__

Say each of these words out loud.

Write the vowel sound you hear.

The first one has been done for you.

cry __i__ sky __i__ try __i__
lazy __e__ oily __e__ funny __e__

The letter y can sometimes work with
a vowel to make a long vowel sound.

Say these words out loud: say they tray way

Learn Together
Discuss the vowel sounds. In the ay words, the y acts
to make the a long. In they, the y does not make a long
e sound. As your child's reading skills develop, they will
notice many other exceptions to general rules.

29

218

Sarge Battles R

Sometimes, other letters can make vowels sound different.

For example, in the word Sarge, a sounds different when followed by r.

The a in Sarge does not sound long or short.

The r changes the sound of the vowel.

Add the missing vowels.

m**a**rbles   b**i**rd   n**u**rse   f**o**rk

c**a**r   tig**e**r   b**a**rn   sk**i**rt

doct**o**r   t**u**rkey   w**o**rd

Say each word out loud.
Listen to the vowel sound.

30

Part of the Team

Sometimes, vowels work together to change a short vowel sound into a long vowel sound.

For example, in the word team, the a helps make the e long.

Say each word out loud. Listen to the vowel sound.

Underline the two words in each row that make the same vowel sound.

sleep	mean	bait
coat	green	deal
soap	feel	boat

32

The letter e at the end of a word can make the vowel in the middle long.

Sam becomes same when you add a silent e.

The short vowel a sound in Sam becomes a long vowel sound.

Add an e to the end of the blue words below.

Help us us**e** the remote.

Plan to make a plan**e**.

The cop can cop**e**.

Take a bit of a bit**e**.

Say these sentences out loud.
Listen to the vowel sounds.

33

Freezing Words

When two consonants work together in a word and you hear both letter sounds, it's called a blend.

For example, the F and r in Frozone make a blend.

Choose a **consonant blend** to make a word.

br tr sl	**br**ick	cl fr bl	**fr**og
fr br sn	**sn**eeze	fl bl cl	**bl**ock
pl st gr	**gr**ain	dr cr st	**st**eam

Answers may vary.
Sample answers are shown.

34

Answers

Page 35

Violet and Dash are using spoons. What is the blend in spoon? **sp**

Answers may vary. Sample answers:

Choose a blend to make a word.

fr   tr   cl   bl   sp   sl

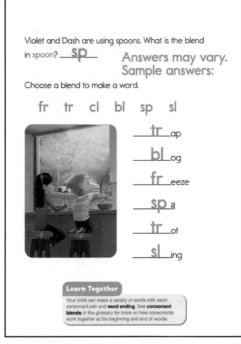

trap
blog
freeze
spill
trot
sling

Learn Together

Your child can make a variety of words with each consonant pair and **word ending**. See **consonant blends** in the glossary for more on how consonants work together at the beginning and end of words.

35

Page 36

Sticking Together to the End

Two or more consonants can also work together at the end of a word.

Hank is Dory's friend.

Listen to the sounds the letters nd make.

Choose one pair of consonants to make a word.

lp nt lt	nt nd mp	st lp rd
he **lp**	ba **nd**	bi **rd**
st pt ct	pt nt mp	lf nt rd
te **st**	la **mp**	elepha **nt**

36

Page 37

Choose one pair of consonants to make a word.

rd   st   nt   nd   mp

Becky is a bi **rd** called a loon.

Dory mu **st** ju **mp** into a drain to escape.

Dory looks differe **nt** from the other fish in the ocean.

Where will Dory's story e **nd** ?

Read the sentences out loud.

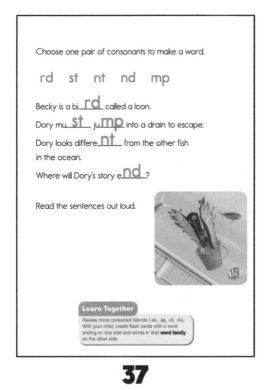

Learn Together

Review more consonant blends (-sk, -sp, -ld, -rk). With your child, create flash cards with a word ending on one side and words in that **word family** on the other side.

37

Page 38

Sticking with Words

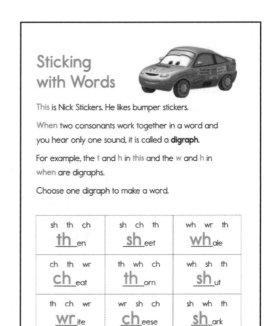

This is Nick Stickers. He likes bumper stickers.

When two consonants work together in a word and you hear only one sound, it is called a **digraph**.

For example, the t and h in this and the w and h in when are digraphs.

Choose one digraph to make a word.

sh th ch	sh ch th	wh wr th
then	**sh**eet	**wh**ale
ch th wr	th wh ch	wh sh th
cheat	**th**orn	**sh**ut
th ch wr	wr sh ch	sh wh th
write	**ch**eese	**sh**ark

38

Read these bumper stickers out loud.

Underline the digraphs.

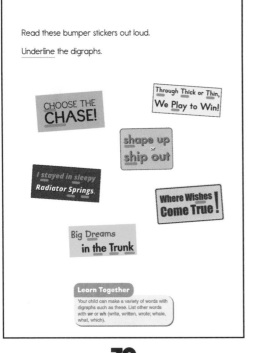

CHOOSE THE
CHASE!

Through Thick or Thin,
We Play to Win!

shape up
or
ship out

I stayed in sleepy
Radiator Springs.

Where Wishes!
Come True!

Big Dreams
in the Trunk

Learn Together
Your child can make a variety of words with digraphs such as these. List other words with **wr** or **wh** (write, written, wrote; whale, what, which).

39

Shhhh!

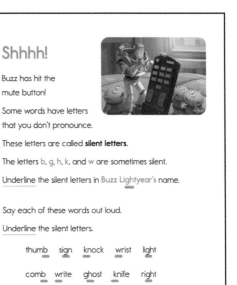

Buzz has hit the
mute button!

Some words have letters
that you don't pronounce.

These letters are called **silent letters**.

The letters b, g, h, k, and w are sometimes silent.

Underline the silent letters in Buzz Lightyear's name.

Say each of these words out loud.

Underline the silent letters.

thumb   sign   knock   wrist   light

comb   write   ghost   knife   right

40

Say each of these words out loud.

Underline the silent letters.

honest   wrist   knight   wrap   gnat

knit   lamb   character   chaos   knee

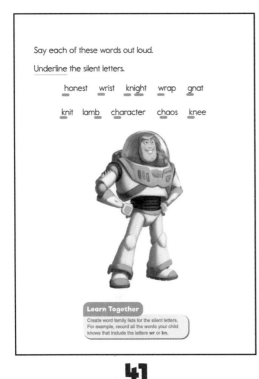

Learn Together
Create word family lists for the silent letters. For example, record all the words your child knows that include the letters **wr** or **kn**.

41

Inside Outside Words

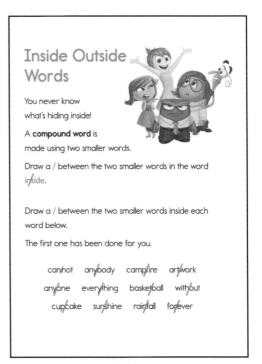

You never know
what's hiding inside!

A **compound word** is
made using two smaller words.

Draw a / between the two smaller words in the word
in/side.

Draw a / between the two smaller words inside each
word below.

The first one has been done for you.

can/not   any/body   camp/fire   art/work

any/one   every/thing   basket/ball   with/out

cup/cake   sun/shine   rain/fall   for/ever

42

Match a word on the left to a word on the right to make a compound word.

finger   bird
home   print
humming   pack
fire   work
back   place

Circle the compound words below.

broomstick   greener   airport   jackpot

forever   jacket   sadness   daycare

Learn Together
Help your child find the little words inside bigger words when reading books together. These little words can often give clues to the meaning of the compound word.

43

Don't Forget, We're Supers

A **contraction** is a word that is made by joining two words.

An apostrophe takes the place of any missing letters.

Match each contraction below with the two words that have been joined.

don't   I am
we're   you are
you're   he is
I'm   do not
he's   we are

44

Fill in the missing contraction to complete each sentence.

__You·re__ about to read an amazing story.

The Incredibles __haven·t__ had any luck lately.

They __can·t__ fly their jet.

__It·s__ broken.

An evil villain is after them. __She·s__ out to get them.

She's
can't
haven't
It's
You're

Use one of the contractions to write a sentence about Supers.

__Answers will vary.__

Learn Together
With your child, create flash cards with a contraction on one side and the two words that form that contraction on the other. Use the cards to play matching games.

45

Not Again but Before

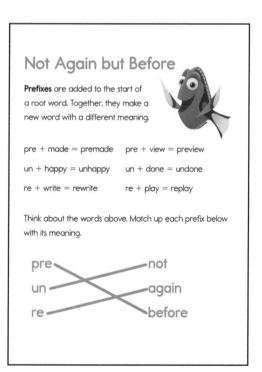

Prefixes are added to the start of a root word. Together, they make a new word with a different meaning.

pre + made = premade   pre + view = preview
un + happy = unhappy   un + done = undone
re + write = rewrite   re + play = replay

Think about the words above. Match up each prefix below with its meaning.

pre   not
un   again
re   before

46

Fill in the missing prefix to complete each sentence below.

You may use each prefix more than once.

Dory is **un**happy when she can't find her parents.

She **re**visits every place she thinks they might be.

Dory is having trouble finding her parents, **un**fortunately.

Will her parents ever **re**appear?

un

re

Add a prefix to a word to make a new word.

un + **do** = **undo**

47

More and Most

Suffixes are added to the end of a word to make a new word.

For example, Lightning McQueen is big, but Taco is bigger. Miss Fritter is the biggest.

Add the root word to its suffix.

Print the new word.

kind + er = **kinder**

kind + est = **kindest**

kind + ness = **kindness**

long + er = **longer**

long + est = **longest**

48

Try adding -er, -est, and -ness to each of the following words.

sweet **sweeter** **sweetest** **sweetness**

soft **softer** **softest** **softness**

hard **harder** **hardest** **hardness**

Think about what each word means.

Label each wheel using small, smaller, smallest.

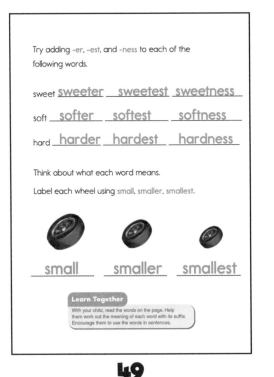

small **smaller** **smallest**

49

Use the correct homophone in each sentence.

We **ate** our lunch together.   ate   eight

I wonder **where** Woody has gone.   wear   where

Bo Peep sees them going over **there**   there   their

What do you want **to** do today?   too   two   to

Why do you **wear** that cowboy hat, Woody?   where   wear

51

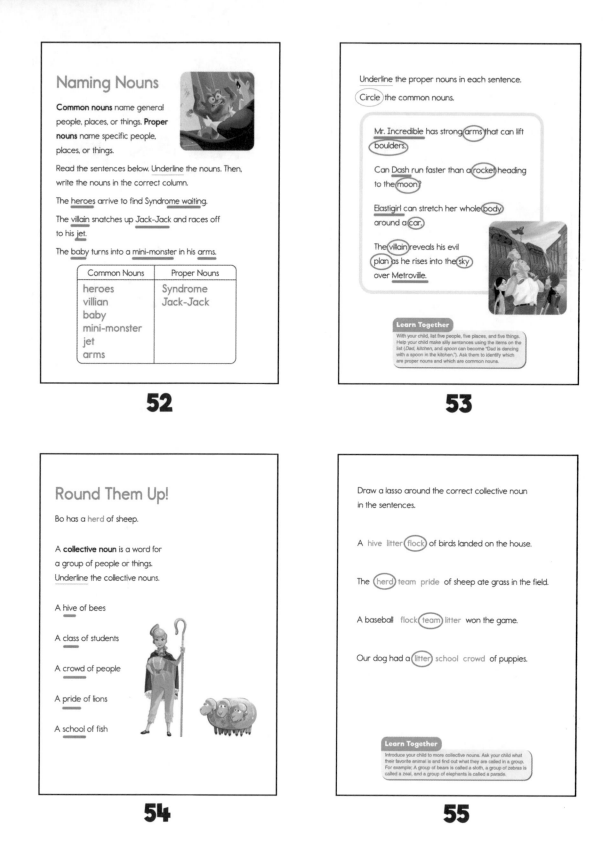

Naming Nouns

Common nouns name general people, places, or things. **Proper nouns** name specific people, places, or things.

Read the sentences below. Underline the nouns. Then, write the nouns in the correct column.

The <u>heroes</u> arrive to find <u>Syndrome</u> waiting.

The <u>villain</u> snatches up <u>Jack-Jack</u> and races off to his <u>jet</u>.

The <u>baby</u> turns into a <u>mini-monster</u> in his <u>arms</u>.

Common Nouns	Proper Nouns
heroes	Syndrome
villian	Jack-Jack
baby	
mini-monster	
jet	
arms	

52

Underline the proper nouns in each sentence. (Circle) the common nouns.

Mr. <u>Incredible</u> has strong (arms) that can lift (boulders.)

Can <u>Dash</u> run faster than a (rocket) heading to the (moon?)

<u>Elastigirl</u> can stretch her whole (body) around a (car.)

The (villain) reveals his evil (plan) as he rises into the (sky) over <u>Metroville</u>.

Learn Together

With your child, list five people, five places, and five things. Help your child make silly sentences using the items on the list (*Dad, kitchen,* and *spoon* can become "Dad is dancing with a spoon in the kitchen."). Ask them to identify which are proper nouns and which are common nouns.

53

Round Them Up!

Bo has a herd of sheep.

A **collective noun** is a word for a group of people or things. Underline the collective nouns.

A <u>hive</u> of bees

A <u>class</u> of students

A <u>crowd</u> of people

A <u>pride</u> of lions

A <u>school</u> of fish

54

Draw a lasso around the correct collective noun in the sentences.

A hive litter (flock) of birds landed on the house.

The (herd) team pride of sheep ate grass in the field.

A baseball flock (team) litter won the game.

Our dog had a (litter) school crowd of puppies.

Learn Together

Introduce your child to more collective nouns. Ask your child what their favorite animal is and find out what they are called in a group. For example: A group of bears is called a sloth, a group of zebras is called a zeal, and a group of elephants is called a parade.

55

Draw a line from each noun to its plural form to help Bo herd them.

tooth — teeth
child — children
goose — geese
foot — feet
sheep — sheep

57

Action!

Underline the **verbs** below.

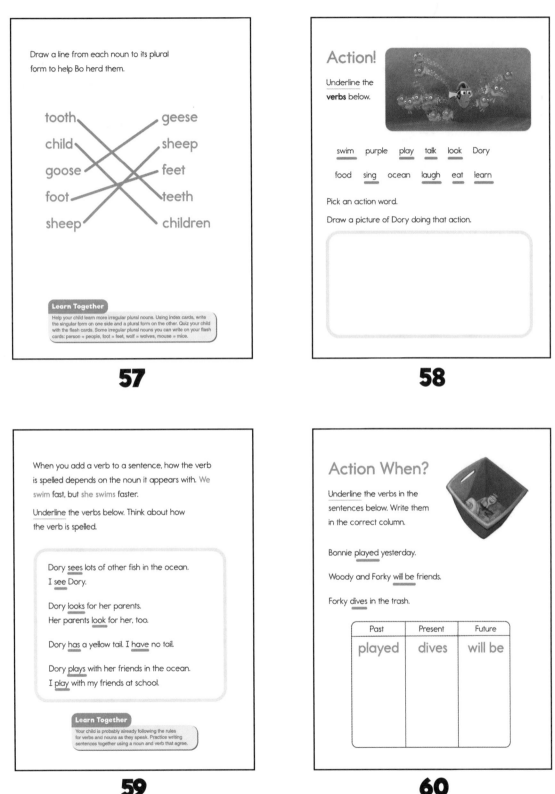

swim   purple   play   talk   look   Dory

food   sing   ocean   laugh   eat   learn

Pick an action word.

Draw a picture of Dory doing that action.

58

When you add a verb to a sentence, how the verb is spelled depends on the noun it appears with. We swim fast, but she swims faster.

Underline the verbs below. Think about how the verb is spelled.

Dory sees lots of other fish in the ocean.
I see Dory.

Dory looks for her parents.
Her parents look for her, too.

Dory has a yellow tail. I have no tail.

Dory plays with her friends in the ocean.
I play with my friends at school.

59

Action When?

Underline the verbs in the sentences below. Write them in the correct column.

Bonnie played yesterday.

Woody and Forky will be friends.

Forky dives in the trash.

Past	Present	Future
played	dives	will be

60

Page 61

Some verbs don't follow the regular spelling pattern. These are called **irregular verbs**.

Underline the irregular verbs in the sentences below. Think about how the verbs are spelled.

> Yesterday: The children <u>woke</u> up. They <u>ate</u> breakfast. They <u>got</u> on the bus. They <u>went</u> to school.
>
> Today: The children <u>wake</u> up. They <u>eat</u> breakfast. They <u>get</u> on the bus. They <u>go</u> to school.

Write another sentence for yesterday using irregular verbs. Answers may vary. Sample answers:

<u>Yesterday, I played outside.</u>

Write another sentence for today using irregular verbs.

<u>Today, I have a karate lesson.</u>

Learn Together
Again, your child is probably already following these rules as they speak. As they write using various **verb tenses**, encourage them to say the sentence to figure out form and spelling. Watch out for irregular verbs.

61

Page 62

Describe It!

An **adjective** is a word that describes a noun.

Riley is happy. The word happy describes Riley.

Add one of these adjectives to a sentence below.

big   friendly   blue

Riley is a <u>f r i e n d l y</u> girl.
Riley's eyes are <u>b l u e</u>.
Riley has a <u>b i g</u> problem.

Write a sentence to describe yourself. Use an adjective.

<u>Answers will vary.</u>

62

Page 63

An **adverb** is a word that describes a verb.

It tells when, where, how, or what.

These are adverbs:
now, loudly, under, inside, carefully.

Riley jumps around happily.

The word happily describes how Riley is jumping.

Add each of these adverbs to a sentence below.

softly   slowly   later   outside

Riley goes <u>o u t s i d e</u> to play.
Riley walks <u>s l o w l y</u>
She whispers <u>s o f t l y</u>
Riley will be happy again <u>l a t e r</u>

Learn Together
Ask your child to describe household items using adjectives. Encourage them to consider color, shapes, smells, and textures. Give your child prompts to complete with adverbs ("The turtle moved _____." "The siren blared _____.").

63

Page 64

A Happy, Cheerful Fish

Synonyms are words with the same or similar meanings.

Dory is a happy, cheerful fish.

Happy and cheerful are synonyms.

Draw a line to match the synonyms.

run — jog
grin — smile
beautiful — pretty
tired — sleepy

64

Dory needs help coming up with synonyms!
Write a new word that has the same or similar meaning as the underlined word.

Answers will vary. Sample answers:

Nemo giggles at Dory's joke. _____ laughs _____

Marlin is a little fish.

_____ small _____

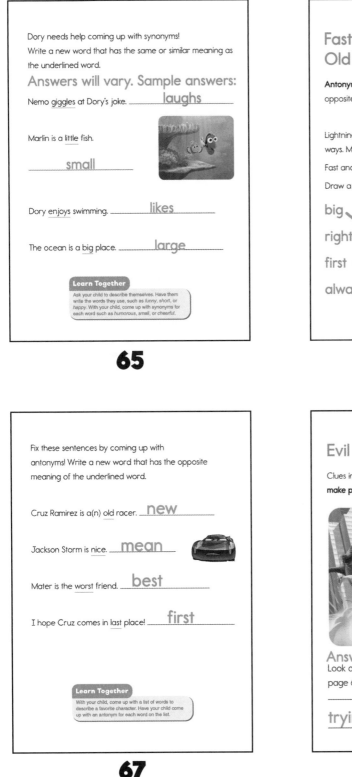

Dory enjoys swimming. _____ likes _____

The ocean is a big place. _____ large _____

Learn Together
Ask your child to describe themselves. Have them write the words they use, such as *funny, short,* or *happy.* With your child, come up with synonyms for each word such as *humorous, small,* or *cheerful.*

65

Fast and Slow, Old and New

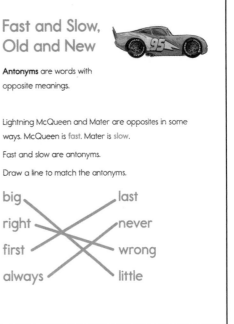

Antonyms are words with opposite meanings.

Lightning McQueen and Mater are opposites in some ways. McQueen is fast. Mater is slow.

Fast and slow are antonyms.

Draw a line to match the antonyms.

big   last
right   never
first   wrong
always   little

66

Fix these sentences by coming up with antonyms! Write a new word that has the opposite meaning of the underlined word.

Cruz Ramirez is a(n) old racer. _____ new

Jackson Storm is nice. _____ mean

Mater is the worst friend. _____ best

I hope Cruz comes in last place! _____ first

Learn Together
With your child, come up with a list of words to describe a favorite character. Have your child come up with an antonym for each word on the list.

67

Evil Robot Attacks City!

Clues in the text and picture can help you **make predictions.**

Answers will vary. Sample answers:
Look at the picture. Predict what the story on page 69 is about.

_____ The Incredibles are all trying to stop an evil robot. _____

68

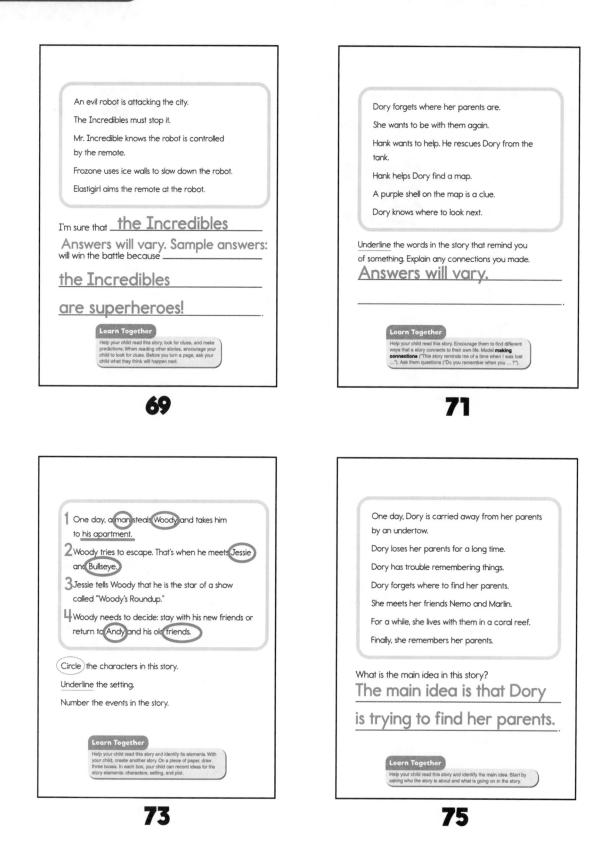

An evil robot is attacking the city.

The Incredibles must stop it.

Mr. Incredible knows the robot is controlled by the remote.

Frozone uses ice walls to slow down the robot.

Elastigirl aims the remote at the robot.

I'm sure that __the Incredibles__

Answers will vary. Sample answers:
will win the battle because _____

the Incredibles

are superheroes!

Learn Together

Help your child read this story, look for clues, and make predictions. When reading other stories, encourage your child to look for clues. Before you turn a page, ask your child what they think will happen next.

69

Dory forgets where her parents are.

She wants to be with them again.

Hank wants to help. He rescues Dory from the tank.

Hank helps Dory find a map.

A purple shell on the map is a clue.

Dory knows where to look next.

Underline the words in the story that remind you of something. Explain any connections you made.

Answers will vary.

_____.

Learn Together

Help your child read this story. Encourage them to find different ways that a story connects to their own life. Model **making connections** ("This story reminds me of a time when I was lost ..."). Ask them questions ("Do you remember when you ... ?").

71

---

1 One day, a man steals Woody and takes him to his apartment.

2 Woody tries to escape. That's when he meets Jessie and Bullseye.

3 Jessie tells Woody that he is the star of a show called "Woody's Roundup."

4 Woody needs to decide: stay with his new friends or return to Andy and his old friends.

Circle the characters in this story.

Underline the setting.

Number the events in the story.

Learn Together

Help your child read this story and identify its elements. With your child, create another story. On a piece of paper, draw three boxes. In each box, your child can record ideas for the story elements: characters, setting, and plot.

73

One day, Dory is carried away from her parents by an undertow.

Dory loses her parents for a long time.

Dory has trouble remembering things.

Dory forgets where to find her parents.

She meets her friends Nemo and Marlin.

For a while, she lives with them in a coral reef.

Finally, she remembers her parents.

What is the main idea in this story?

The main idea is that Dory

is trying to find her parents.

Learn Together

Help your child read this story and identify the main idea. Start by asking who the story is about and what is going on in the story.

75

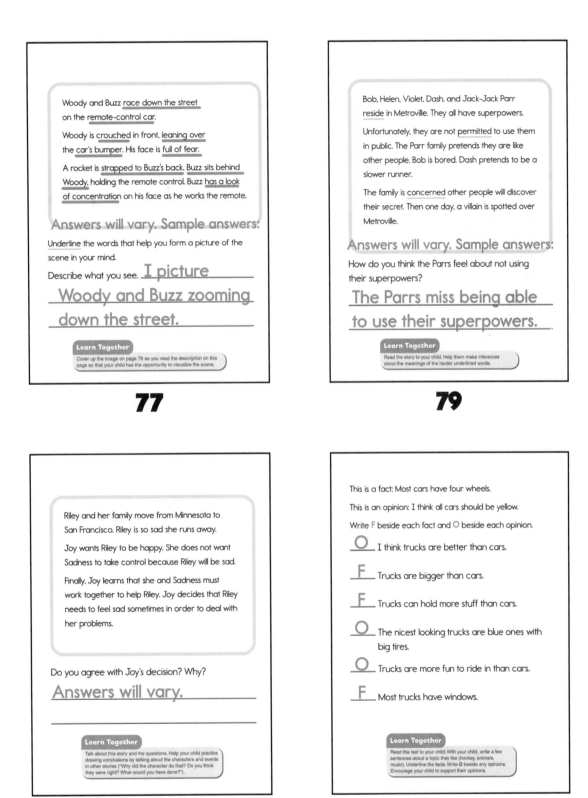

Woody and Buzz <u>race down the street</u>
on the remote-control car.

Woody is <u>crouched in front</u>, <u>leaning over</u>
<u>the car's bumper</u>. <u>His face is full of fear</u>.

A rocket is <u>strapped to Buzz's back</u>. Buzz sits behind
<u>Woody</u>, holding the remote control. <u>Buzz has a look</u>
<u>of concentration</u> on his face as he works the remote.

Answers will vary. Sample answers:

Underline the words that help you form a picture of the
scene in your mind.

Describe what you see. **I picture**
Woody and Buzz zooming
down the street.

Learn Together
Cover up the image on page 76 as you read the description on this
page so that your child has the opportunity to visualize the scene.

77

Bob, Helen, Violet, Dash, and Jack-Jack Parr
<u>reside</u> in Metroville. They all have superpowers.

Unfortunately, they are not <u>permitted</u> to use them
in public. The Parr family pretends they are like
other people. Bob is bored. Dash pretends to be a
slower runner.

The family is <u>concerned</u> other people will discover
their secret. Then one day, a villain is spotted over
Metroville.

Answers will vary. Sample answers:

How do you think the Parrs feel about not using
their superpowers?

The Parrs miss being able
to use their superpowers.

Learn Together
Read the story to your child. Help them make inferences
about the meanings of the harder underlined words.

79

Riley and her family move from Minnesota to
San Francisco. Riley is so sad she runs away.

Joy wants Riley to be happy. She does not want
Sadness to take control because Riley will be sad.

Finally, Joy learns that she and Sadness must
work together to help Riley. Joy decides that Riley
needs to feel sad sometimes in order to deal with
her problems.

Do you agree with Joy's decision? Why?

Answers will vary.

Learn Together
Talk about this story and the questions. Help your child practice
drawing conclusions by talking about the characters and events
in other stories ("Why did the character do that? Do you think
they were right? What would you have done?").

81

This is a fact: Most cars have four wheels.

This is an opinion: I think all cars should be yellow.

Write F beside each fact and O beside each opinion.

O I think trucks are better than cars.

F Trucks are bigger than cars.

F Trucks can hold more stuff than cars.

O The nicest looking trucks are blue ones with
big tires.

O Trucks are more fun to ride in than cars.

F Most trucks have windows.

Learn Together
Read this text to your child. With your child, write a few
sentences about a topic they like (hockey, animals,
music). Underline the facts. Write O beside any opinions.
Encourage your child to support their opinions.

83

Answers

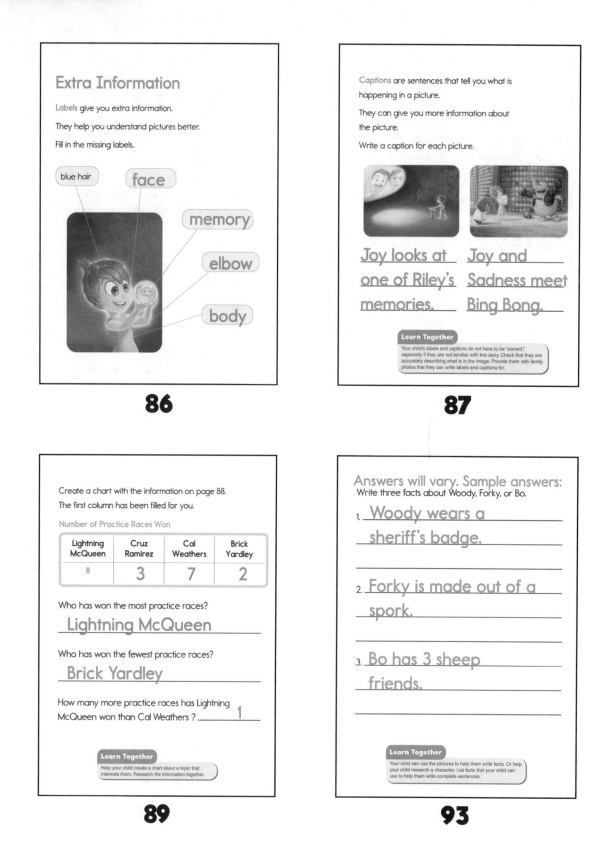

Extra Information

Labels give you extra information.

They help you understand pictures better.

Fill in the missing labels.

blue hair

face

memory

elbow

body

86

Captions are sentences that tell you what is happening in a picture.

They can give you more information about the picture.

Write a caption for each picture.

Joy looks at one of Riley's memories.

Joy and Sadness meet Bing Bong.

Learn Together
Your child's labels and captions do not have to be "correct," especially if they are not familiar with this story. Check that they are accurately describing what is in the image. Provide them with family photos that they can write labels and captions for.

87

Create a chart with the information on page 88.

The first column has been filled for you.

Number of Practice Races Won

Lightning McQueen	Cruz Ramirez	Cal Weathers	Brick Yardley
8	3	7	2

Who has won the most practice races?

Lightning McQueen

Who has won the fewest practice races?

Brick Yardley

How many more practice races has Lightning McQueen won than Cal Weathers ? ___1___

Learn Together
Help your child create a chart about a topic that interests them. Research the information together.

89

Answers will vary. Sample answers:
Write three facts about Woody, Forky, or Bo.

1. Woody wears a sheriff's badge.

2. Forky is made out of a spork.

3. Bo has 3 sheep friends.

Learn Together
Your child can use the pictures to help them write facts. Or help your child research a character. List facts that your child can use to help them write complete sentences.

93

230

Capitalize That!

The names of holidays, products, and specific places need to be capitalized.

Earth Day

Fluke's Fish Flakes

Marine Life Institute

Circle the holidays, products, and places that should be capitalized.

(thanksgiving)   pencil

(newport aquarium)   dolphin

(april fool's day)   (chum's chocolate)

94

Rewrite the sentences with the correct capitalization.

my pet fish is from bob's fish mart.

<u>My pet fish is from Bob's</u>
<u>Fish Mart.</u>

i got her for christmas.

<u>I got her for Christmas.</u>
_____

she loves to eat fluke's fish flakes!

<u>She loves to eat Fluke's</u>
<u>Fish Flakes!</u>

Learn Together
Practice more capitalization with your child. Have them write the names of their favorite breakfast cereal, favorite holiday, and somewhere they'd like to go on vacation.

95

Writing Sentences

Sentences end in different types of punctuation.

Bob Parr is bored by his job.

> A sentence that ends with a period is telling you something.

How will Mr. Incredible defeat Syndrome?

> A sentence that ends with a question mark is asking a question.

Answers will vary.

Write a sentence about the Incredibles that ends with a period or question mark. _____

<u>The Incredibles are superheroes.</u>

96

The Incredibles are trapped!

> A sentence that ends with an exclamation mark can show excitement or surprise.

Save the family, Violet!

> An exclamation mark at the end of a sentence can also be a command.

Answers will vary.

Write a sentence about the Incredibles that ends with an exclamation mark.

<u>The Incredibles</u>

<u>save the day!</u>

Learn Together
With your child, take turns writing sentences about yourselves that end with different punctuation marks. Remind them to use a capital letter at the beginning of each sentence.

97

Page 99

Rewrite the sentences below and add the missing commas.

I like to eat cereal apples and toast.

I like to eat cereal, apples, and toast.

After eating I brush my teeth.

After eating, I brush my teeth.

If you ride a bike you should wear a helmet.

If you ride a bike, you should wear a helmet.

My favorite colors are orange red and purple.

My favorite colors are orange, red, and purple.

Learn Together
Help your child write a letter to their favorite character. With your child, review sentences in the letter, looking for opportunities to include commas or other punctuation they are learning about.

99

Page 100

Belonging and More

An apostrophe can be used to show possession.
This is an apostrophe: '

Nemo is Marlin's son.

Dory's friends are Marlin, Nemo, Hank, Destiny, and Bailey.

Add an apostrophe to each sentence.

Dory's parents set out shell trails.

Hank's arms are really long.

100

Page 101

A contraction is two words put together.
The missing letters are replaced by an apostrophe.
For example, is not becomes isn't.

Make contractions with the words below, adding an apostrophe.

I have __I've__   we will __we'll__

we are __we're__   they have __they've__

let us __let's__   you are __you're__

he is __he's__   she is __she's__

should not __shouldn't__ would not __wouldn't__

Learn Together
Help your child list more contractions. Look for contractions in a story. Have your child point them out and say the two words that make the contraction.

101

Page 104

Speed Counts

How fast can Lightning McQueen go?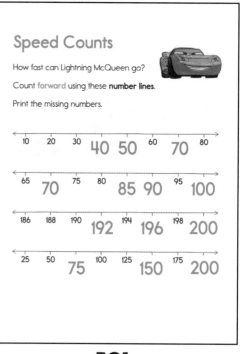
Count forward using these **number lines**.
Print the missing numbers.

10 20 30 **40 50** 60 **70** 80

65 **70** 75 80 **85 90** 95 **100**

186 188 190 **192** 194 **196** 198 **200**

25 50 **75** 100 125 **150** 175 **200**

104

Print the missing numbers on the **100-chart**.

100	101	102	103	104	105	106	107	108	109
110	111	112	113	114	115	116	117	118	119
120	121	122	123	124	125	126	127	128	129
130	131	132	133	134	135	136	137	138	139
140	141	142	143	144	145	146	147	148	149
150	151	152	153	154	155	156	157	158	159
160	161	162	163	164	165	166	167	168	169
170	171	172	173	174	175	176	177	178	179
180	181	182	183	184	185	186	187	188	189
190	191	192	193	194	195	196	197	198	199

Learn Together

Find opportunities to practice **skip counting** to 1,000, either by twos, fives, or tens. While counting, you might play hide-and-seek together, bounce a ball, or jump rope.

105

Countdown!

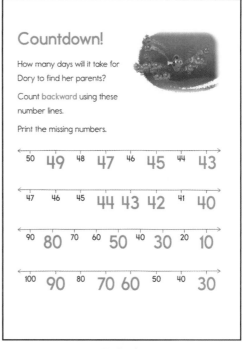

How many days will it take for Dory to find her parents?

Count backward using these number lines.

Print the missing numbers.

50 49 48 47 46 45 44 43

47 46 45 44 43 42 41 40

90 80 70 60 50 40 30 20 10

100 90 80 70 60 50 40 30

106

Print the missing numbers on the 100-chart.

100	99	98	97	96	95	94	93	92	91
90	89	88	87	86	85	84	83	82	81
80	79	78	77	76	75	74	73	72	71
70	69	68	67	66	65	64	63	62	61
60	59	58	57	56	55	54	53	52	51
50	49	48	47	46	45	44	43	42	41
40	39	38	37	36	35	34	33	32	31
30	29	28	27	26	25	24	23	22	21
20	19	18	17	16	15	14	13	12	11
10	9	8	7	6	5	4	3	2	1

Learn Together

Cover up numbers on the 100-chart, encouraging your child to count backward and identify the missing numbers. With your child, create number lines to use for other simple problems.

107

Super Frames

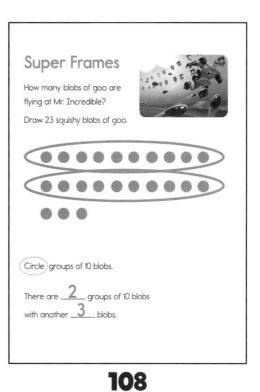

How many blobs of goo are flying at Mr. Incredible?

Draw 23 squishy blobs of goo.

(Circle) groups of 10 blobs.

There are ___2___ groups of 10 blobs with another ___3___ blobs.

108

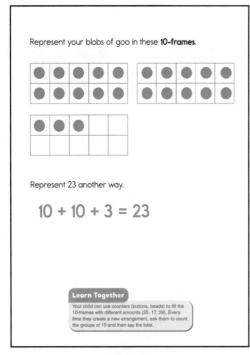

Represent your blobs of goo in these **10-frames**.

Represent 23 another way.

$$10 + 10 + 3 = 23$$

Learn Together
Your child can use counters (buttons, beads) to fill the 10-frames with different amounts (25, 17, 29). Every time they create a new arrangement, ask them to count the groups of 10 and then say the total.

109

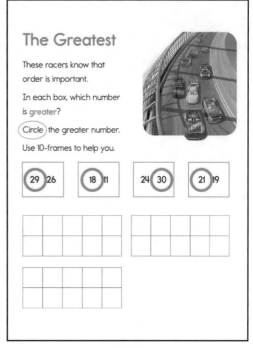

The Greatest

These racers know that order is important.

In each box, which number is greater?

Circle the greater number.

Use 10-frames to help you.

29 26   18 11   24 30   21 19

110

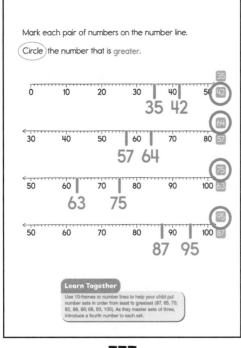

Mark each pair of numbers on the number line.

Circle the number that is greater.

35 42

57 64

63 75

87 95

Learn Together
Use 10-frames or number lines to help your child put number sets in order from least to greatest (87, 65, 70; 82, 99, 86; 66, 83, 100). As they master sets of three, introduce a fourth number to each set.

111

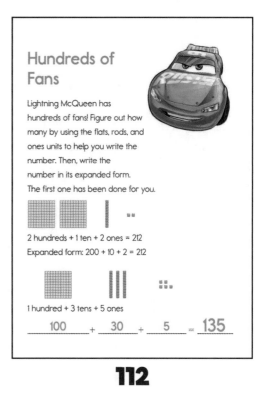

Hundreds of Fans

Lightning McQueen has hundreds of fans! Figure out how many by using the flats, rods, and ones units to help you write the number. Then, write the number in its expanded form. The first one has been done for you.

2 hundreds + 1 ten + 2 ones = 212
Expanded form: 200 + 10 + 2 = 212

1 hundred + 3 tens + 5 ones

$$100 + 30 + 5 = 135$$

112

113

Write the number!

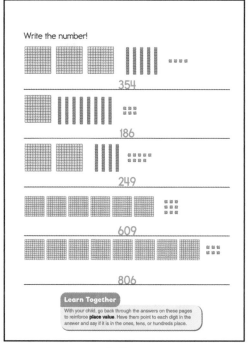

354

186

249

609

806

114

Quick Comparisons

Can you be as fast as Dash?

Write >, <, or = to compare.

460 < 540   157 > 120

575 < 590   918 > 908

837 > 825   432 < 471

115

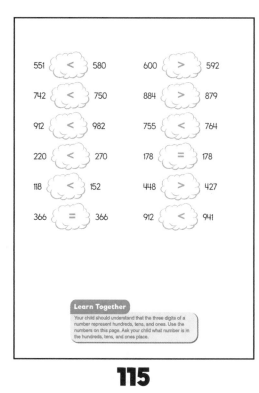

551 < 580   600 > 592

742 < 750   884 > 879

912 < 982   755 < 764

220 < 270   178 = 178

118 < 152   448 > 427

366 = 366   912 < 941

116

We're Rich!

Woody and Buzz are counting money.

Draw a line from the money to its value.

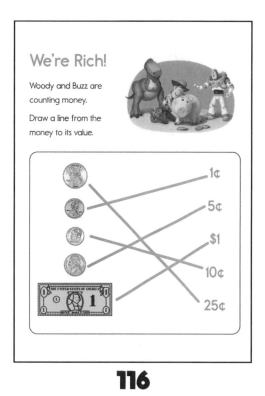

1¢

5¢

$1

10¢

25¢

117

Show 25¢ in 2 ways.

Answers will vary. Sample answers:

1 quarter	2 dimes and 1 nickel

Show 50¢ in 2 ways.

2 quarters	5 dimes

Show $1 in 2 ways.

4 quarters	10 dimes

Learn Together
Work with your child to figure out other ways to show these amounts. Use coins to help them.

118

Just a Fraction

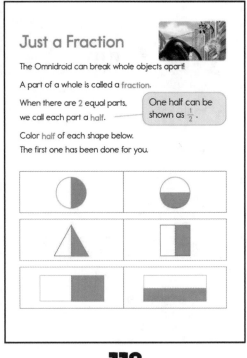

The Omnidroid can break whole objects apart!

A part of a whole is called a fraction.

When there are 2 equal parts, we call each part a half.

> One half can be shown as $\frac{1}{2}$.

Color half of each shape below.
The first one has been done for you.

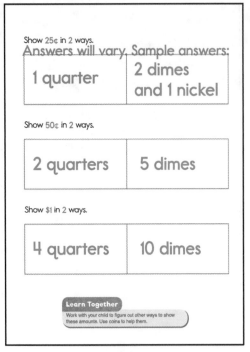

119

When there are 4 equal parts, we call each part a fourth or a quarter.

> One quarter can be shown as $\frac{1}{4}$.

Color one fourth of each shape below.

The first one has been done for you.

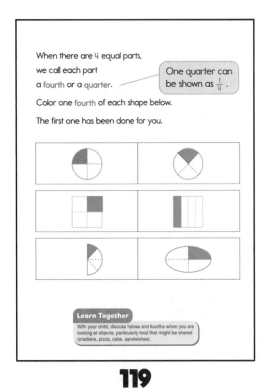

Learn Together
With your child, discuss halves and fourths when you are looking at objects, particularly food that might be shared (crackers, pizza, cake, sandwiches).

120

Part of a Whole

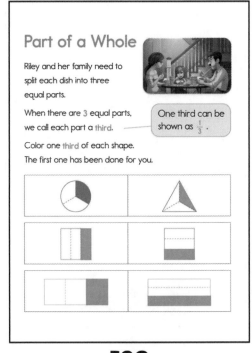

Riley and her family need to split each dish into three equal parts.

When there are 3 equal parts, we call each part a third.

> One third can be shown as $\frac{1}{3}$.

Color one third of each shape.
The first one has been done for you.

This bar is 8 blocks long.

Split the bar in half.

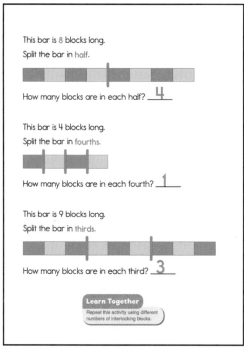

How many blocks are in each half? __4__

This bar is 4 blocks long.

Split the bar in fourths.

How many blocks are in each fourth? __1__

This bar is 9 blocks long.

Split the bar in thirds.

How many blocks are in each third? __3__

Learn Together
Repeat this activity using different numbers of interlocking blocks.

121

Over and Over

Patterns repeat over and over. Spot the pattern in this picture.

Draw the part of each pattern that repeats over and over.

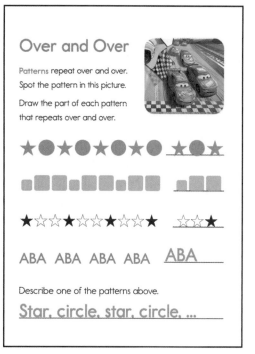

★●★●★●★● ★●★

▪▪▪▪▪▪▪▪ ▪▪▪

★☆★☆★☆★☆★ ☆☆★

ABA ABA ABA ABA __ABA__

Describe one of the patterns above.

__Star, circle, star, circle, ...__

122

Patterns can change by size, shape, color, or direction.

Draw the part of each pattern that repeats.

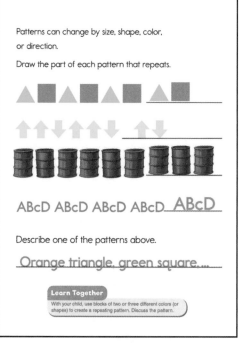

▲■▲■▲■ ▲■

↑↓↑↓↑↓ ↑↓

ABcD ABcD ABcD ABcD __ABcD__

Describe one of the patterns above.

__Orange triangle, green square, ...__

Learn Together
With your child, use blocks of two or three different colors (or shapes) to create a repeating pattern. Discuss the pattern.

123

Colorful Patterns

What patterns do you see in this picture?

Finish each of the patterns below by adding color.

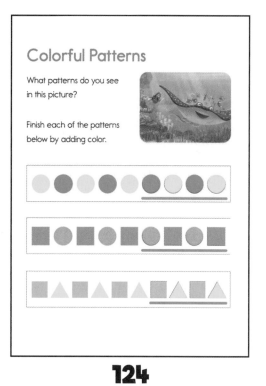

124

Growing and Shrinking

Extend each pattern.

Circle if the pattern is shrinking or growing.

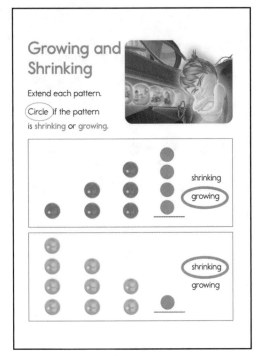

shrinking
(growing)

(shrinking)
growing

Extend each pattern.

Circle if the pattern is shrinking or growing.

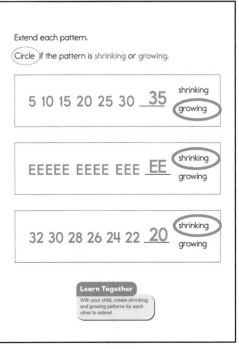

5 10 15 20 25 30 __35__   shrinking (growing)

EEEEE EEEE EEE __EE__   (shrinking) growing

32 30 28 26 24 22 __20__   (shrinking) growing

Learn Together
With your child, create shrinking and growing patterns for each other to extend.

126

127

Skipping Along

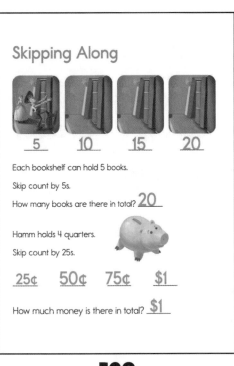

__5__   __10__   __15__   __20__

Each bookshelf can hold 5 books.

Skip count by 5s.

How many books are there in total? __20__

Hamm holds 4 quarters.

Skip count by 25s.

__25¢__   __50¢__   __75¢__   __$1__

How much money is there in total? __$1__

Find the next 3 numbers.

25, 30, __35__ , __40__ , __45__

20, 30, __40__ , __50__ , __60__

100, 200, __300__ , __400__ , __500__

600, 700, __800__ , __900__ , __1000__

50, 60, __70__ , __80__ , __90__

45, 50, __55__ , __60__ , __65__

80, 90, __100__ , __110__ , __120__

Learn Together
Make number lines of different intervals to help your child practice skip counting.

128

129

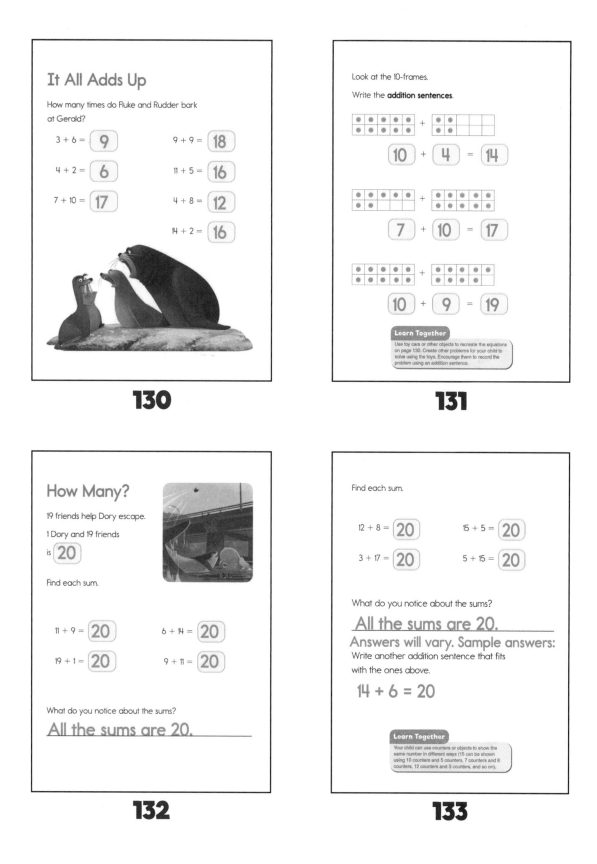

It All Adds Up

How many times do Fluke and Rudder bark at Gerald?

$3 + 6 =$ 9 $9 + 9 =$ 18

$4 + 2 =$ 6 $11 + 5 =$ 16

$7 + 10 =$ 17 $4 + 8 =$ 12

$14 + 2 =$ 16

130

Look at the 10-frames.

Write the **addition sentences**.

10 + 4 = 14

7 + 10 = 17

10 + 9 = 19

Learn Together

Use toy cars or other objects to recreate the equations on page 130. Create other problems for your child to solve using the toys. Encourage them to record the problem using an addition sentence.

131

How Many?

19 friends help Dory escape.

1 Dory and 19 friends is 20

Find each sum.

$11 + 9 =$ 20 $6 + 14 =$ 20

$19 + 1 =$ 20 $9 + 11 =$ 20

What do you notice about the sums?

All the sums are 20.

132

Find each sum.

$12 + 8 =$ 20 $15 + 5 =$ 20

$3 + 17 =$ 20 $5 + 15 =$ 20

What do you notice about the sums?

All the sums are 20.

Answers will vary. Sample answers:
Write another addition sentence that fits with the ones above.

$14 + 6 = 20$

Learn Together

Your child can use counters or objects to show the same number in different ways (15 can be shown using 10 counters and 5 counters, 7 counters and 8 counters, 12 counters and 3 counters, and so on).

133

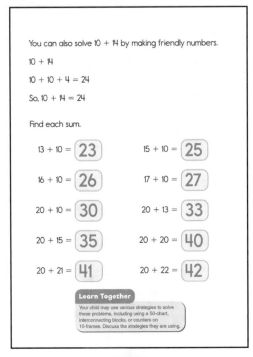

You can also solve 10 + 14 by making friendly numbers.

10 + 14

10 + 10 + 4 = 24

So, 10 + 14 = 24

Find each sum.

13 + 10 = [23]   15 + 10 = [25]

16 + 10 = [26]   17 + 10 = [27]

20 + 10 = [30]   20 + 13 = [33]

20 + 15 = [35]   20 + 20 = [40]

20 + 21 = [41]   20 + 22 = [42]

Learn Together
Your child may use various strategies to solve these problems, including using a 50-chart, interconnecting blocks, or counters on 10-frames. Discuss the strategies they are using.

135

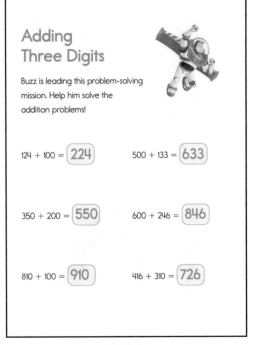

Adding Three Digits

Buzz is leading this problem-solving mission. Help him solve the addition problems!

124 + 100 = [224]   500 + 133 = [633]

350 + 200 = [550]   600 + 246 = [846]

810 + 100 = [910]   416 + 310 = [726]

136

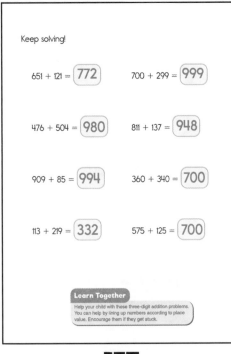

Keep solving!

651 + 121 = [772]   700 + 299 = [999]

476 + 504 = [980]   811 + 137 = [948]

909 + 85 = [994]   360 + 340 = [700]

113 + 219 = [332]   575 + 125 = [700]

Learn Together
Help your child with these three-digit addition problems. You can help by lining up numbers according to place value. Encourage them if they get stuck.

137

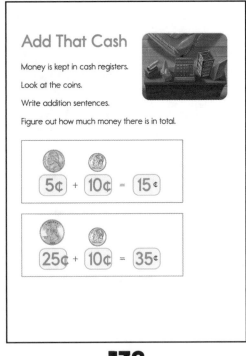

Add That Cash

Money is kept in cash registers.

Look at the coins.

Write addition sentences.

Figure out how much money there is in total.

[5¢] + [10¢] = [15¢]

[25¢] + [10¢] = [35¢]

138

Look at the coins.

Estimate, then find the total.

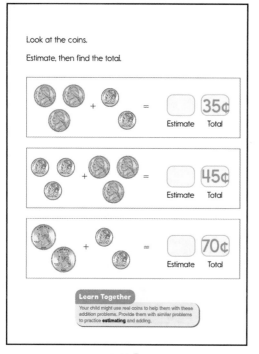

Estimate [ ] Total 35¢

Estimate [ ] Total 45¢

Estimate [ ] Total 70¢

139

I "Otter" Take Some Away

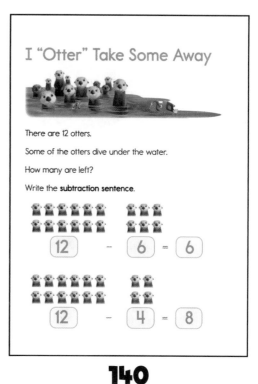

There are 12 otters.

Some of the otters dive under the water.

How many are left?

Write the **subtraction sentence**.

12 − 6 = 6

12 − 4 = 8

140

Look at the 10-frames.

Write the subtraction sentences.

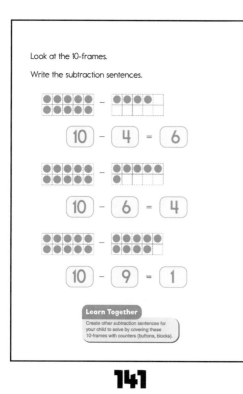

10 − 4 = 6

10 − 6 = 4

10 − 9 = 1

141

What's Left?

There are 4 toys all together.

Then, 1 toy falls.

How many are left?

4 − 1 = 3

Subtract to find each difference.

9 − 1 = 8   7 − 3 = 4

14 − 1 = 13   8 − 3 = 5

18 − 4 = 14   12 − 4 = 8

17 − 4 = 13   16 − 4 = 12

142

There are 5 toys all together.

1 toy leaves.

How many are left?

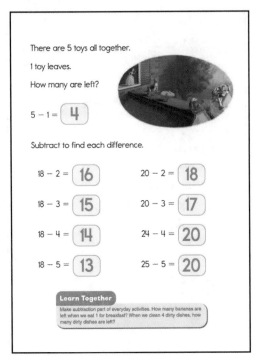

$5 - 1 = \boxed{4}$

Subtract to find each difference.

$18 - 2 = \boxed{16}$ $20 - 2 = \boxed{18}$

$18 - 3 = \boxed{15}$ $20 - 3 = \boxed{17}$

$18 - 4 = \boxed{14}$ $24 - 4 = \boxed{20}$

$18 - 5 = \boxed{13}$ $25 - 5 = \boxed{20}$

Learn Together
Make subtraction part of everyday activities. How many bananas are left when we eat 1 for breakfast? When we clean 4 dirty dishes, how many dirty dishes are left?

143

Find each difference.

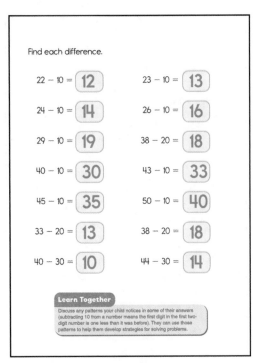

$22 - 10 = \boxed{12}$ $23 - 10 = \boxed{13}$

$24 - 10 = \boxed{14}$ $26 - 10 = \boxed{16}$

$29 - 10 = \boxed{19}$ $38 - 20 = \boxed{18}$

$40 - 10 = \boxed{30}$ $43 - 10 = \boxed{33}$

$45 - 10 = \boxed{35}$ $50 - 10 = \boxed{40}$

$33 - 20 = \boxed{13}$ $38 - 20 = \boxed{18}$

$40 - 30 = \boxed{10}$ $44 - 30 = \boxed{14}$

Learn Together
Discuss any patterns your child notices in some of their answers (subtracting 10 from a number means the first digit in the first two-digit number is one less than it was before). They can use those patterns to help them develop strategies for solving problems.

145

Take It Away!

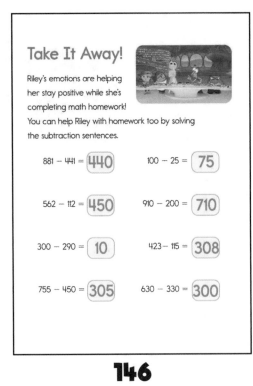

Riley's emotions are helping her stay positive while she's completing math homework!

You can help Riley with homework too by solving the subtraction sentences.

$881 - 441 = \boxed{440}$ $100 - 25 = \boxed{75}$

$562 - 112 = \boxed{450}$ $910 - 200 = \boxed{710}$

$300 - 290 = \boxed{10}$ $423 - 115 = \boxed{308}$

$755 - 450 = \boxed{305}$ $630 - 330 = \boxed{300}$

146

Solve these subtraction sentences.

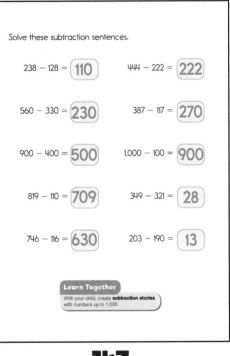

$238 - 128 = \boxed{110}$ $444 - 222 = \boxed{222}$

$560 - 330 = \boxed{230}$ $387 - 117 = \boxed{270}$

$900 - 400 = \boxed{500}$ $1,000 - 100 = \boxed{900}$

$819 - 110 = \boxed{709}$ $349 - 321 = \boxed{28}$

$746 - 116 = \boxed{630}$ $203 - 190 = \boxed{13}$

Learn Together
With your child, create **subtraction stories** with numbers up to 1,000.

147

Less Cash

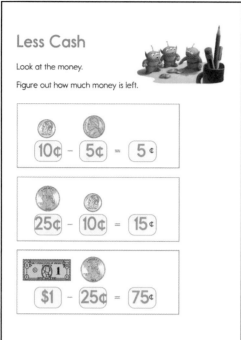

Look at the money.

Figure out how much money is left.

10¢ − 5¢ = 5 ¢

25¢ − 10¢ = 15 ¢

$1 − 25¢ = 75 ¢

Look at the money.

Figure out how much money is left.

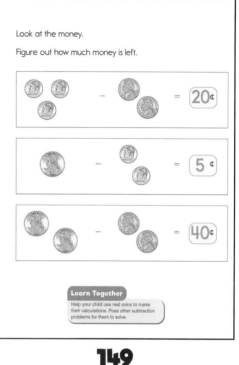

− = 20¢

− = 5 ¢

− = 40¢

Learn Together

Help your child use real coins to make their calculations. Pose other subtraction problems for them to solve.

148   **149**

Adding Up and Taking Away

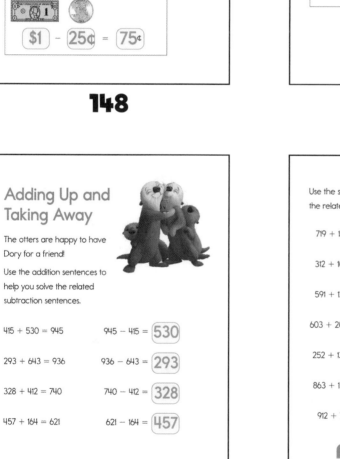

The otters are happy to have Dory for a friend!

Use the addition sentences to help you solve the related subtraction sentences.

415 + 530 = 945   945 − 415 = 530

293 + 643 = 936   936 − 643 = 293

328 + 412 = 740   740 − 412 = 328

457 + 164 = 621   621 − 164 = 457

Use the subtraction sentences to help you solve the related addition sentences.

719 + 182 = 901   901 − 719 = 182

312 + 105 = 417   417 − 105 = 312

591 + 120 = 711   711 − 120 = 591

603 + 209 = 812   812 − 209 = 603

252 + 130 = 382   382 − 252 = 130

863 + 137 = 1,000   1,000 − 863 = 137

912 + 78 = 990   990 − 78 = 912

Learn Together

Help your child to see how each addition sentence is related to a subtraction sentence, and vice versa. Use blocks or toys to show the relationship for one set of sentences.

150   **151**

Some Super Humans

Dash is running late for school and needs quick homework help! Help him solve the addition and subtraction **word problems**.

Nasim and Miguel like to recycle. Nasim found and recycled 46 bottles. Miguel found and recycled 31 bottles.

How many bottles did they recycle in all?

$$46 + 31 = \boxed{77}$$

152

Keep helping Dash solve the problems!

My school has a goal to plant 100 trees in one year. So far, we have planted 58.

How many more trees do we have to plant to reach our goal?

$$100 - 58 = \boxed{42}$$

Jayden is trying to use less water when he showers. During his first shower he saves 15 gallons of water. During his second shower he saves 27 gallons of water.

How many gallons of water has he saved in all?

$$15 + 27 = \boxed{42}$$

Learn Together

Help your child practice more addition and subtraction word problems about their everyday life. Ask them questions like, "If you ride your bike for 23 minutes today and 50 minutes tomorrow, how many minutes will you ride your bike in all?" Be sure the answers are within 100.

153

It Takes Two!

Some word problems ask you to solve two equations.

Solve the two-step word problems.
You might need addition and subtraction for some!

Dory is counting fish in the aquarium.

In one tank, she counts 10 purple fish.

In another tank, she counts 75 black fish.

In another tank, she counts 29 blue fish.

How many fish did Dory count in all?

114

154

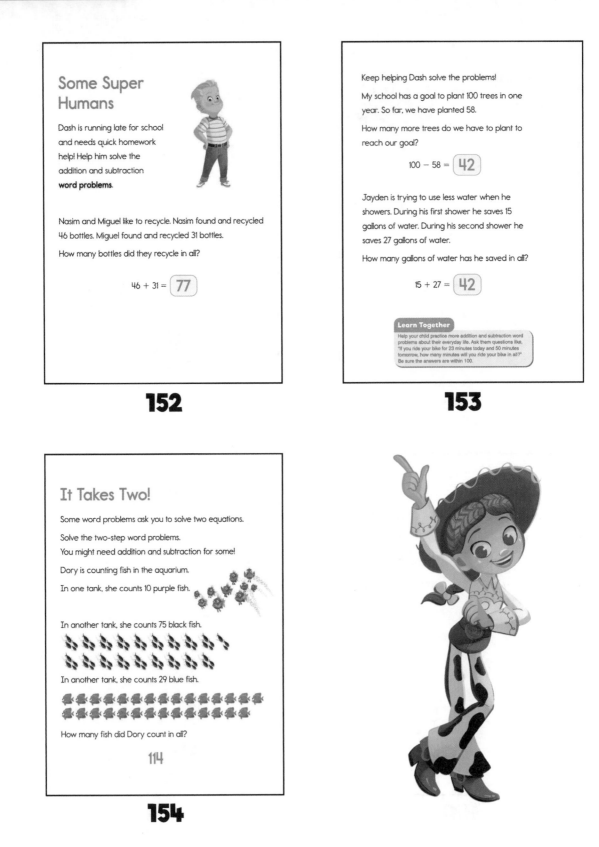

Page 155

Solve more two-step word problems.

Dory loves shells. She collected 23 shells on Monday, 67 shells on Tuesday, and 48 shells on Wednesday.

How many more shells did she collect on Monday and Wednesday than on Tuesday?

4

There are 84 seals resting on the shore. First, 31 seals leave to hunt fish. Then, 52 more seals leave to hunt fish.

How many seals are left on shore?

1

Learn Together

Help your child practice more two-step word problems about their everyday life. For example, you have to bake 60 cookies for the bake sale. If you bake 24 chocolate chip cookies and 28 peanut butter cookies, how many more cookies do you need to bake?

155

Page 157

Count and write the number for each group of masks. Then, label the groups odd or even.

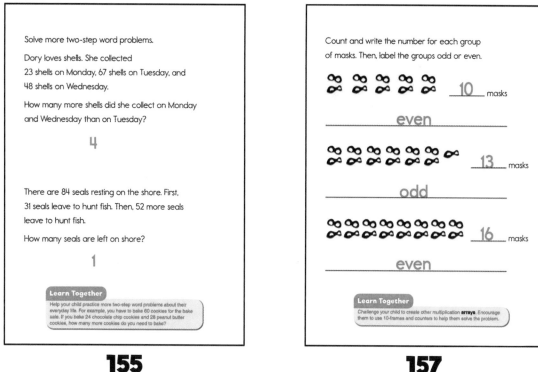

___10___ masks

even

___13___ masks

odd

___16___ masks

even

Learn Together

Challenge your child to create other multiplication **arrays**. Encourage them to use 10-frames and counters to help them solve the problem.

157

Joining Equal Groups

You multiply when you join equal groups.

Here are 4 groups of 2 fish.

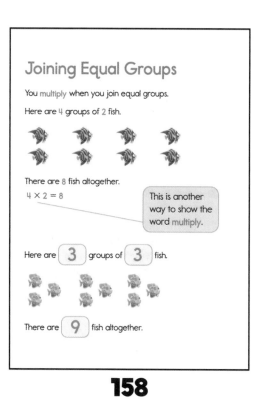

There are 8 fish altogether.

$4 \times 2 = 8$

This is another way to show the word multiply.

Here are [3] groups of [3] fish.

There are [9] fish altogether.

158

Page 159

Here are [3] groups of [4] fish.

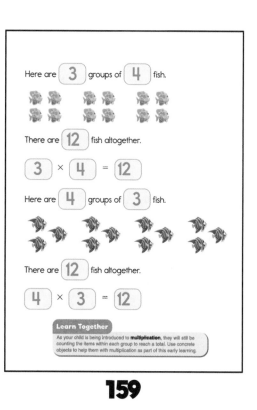

There are [12] fish altogether.

[3] × [4] = [12]

Here are [4] groups of [3] fish.

There are [12] fish altogether.

[4] × [3] = [12]

Learn Together

As your child is being introduced to **multiplication**, they will still be counting the items within each group to reach a total. Use concrete objects to help them with multiplication as part of this early learning.

159

Let's Multiply

Flo has many barrels of oil. You can multiply to find out how many she has.

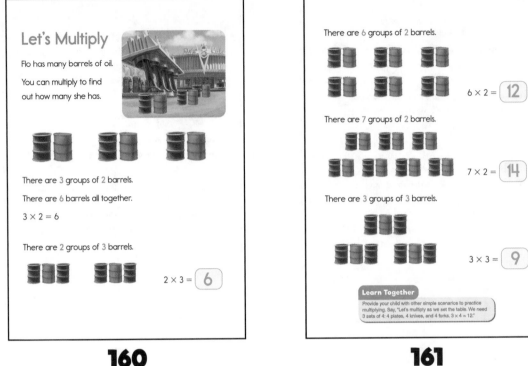

There are 3 groups of 2 barrels.

There are 6 barrels all together.

$3 \times 2 = 6$

There are 2 groups of 3 barrels.

$2 \times 3 = \boxed{6}$

160

There are 6 groups of 2 barrels.

$6 \times 2 = \boxed{12}$

There are 7 groups of 2 barrels.

$7 \times 2 = \boxed{14}$

There are 3 groups of 3 barrels.

$3 \times 3 = \boxed{9}$

Learn Together

Provide your child with other simple scenarios to practice multiplying. Say, "Let's multiply as we set the table. We need 3 sets of 4: 4 plates, 4 knives, and 4 forks. $3 \times 4 = 12$."

161

Separating Equal Groups

You divide when you want to share a group in equal parts.

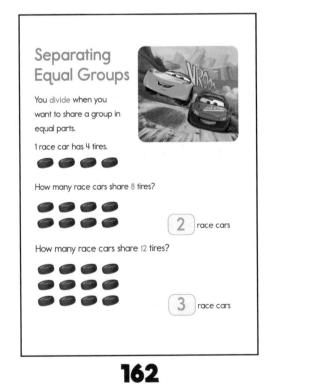

1 race car has 4 tires.

How many race cars share 8 tires?

$\boxed{2}$ race cars

How many race cars share 12 tires?

$\boxed{3}$ race cars

162

How many race cars share 16 tires?

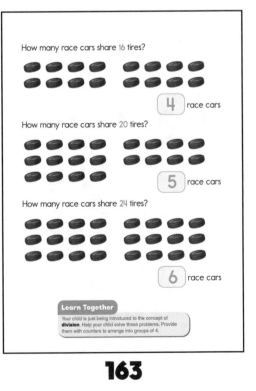

$\boxed{4}$ race cars

How many race cars share 20 tires?

$\boxed{5}$ race cars

How many race cars share 24 tires?

$\boxed{6}$ race cars

Learn Together

Your child is just being introduced to the concept of **division**. Help your child solve these problems. Provide them with counters to arrange into groups of 4.

163

(Circle) groups of Green Army Men to show each division sentence

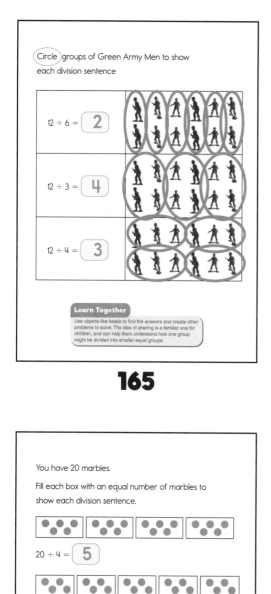

$12 \div 6 = \boxed{2}$

$12 \div 3 = \boxed{4}$

$12 \div 4 = \boxed{3}$

Learn Together
Use objects like beads to find the answers and create other problems to solve. The idea of sharing is a familiar one for children, and can help them understand how one group might be divided into smaller equal groups.

165

Making Equal Groups

Show how the 10 fish below can be divided equally into 2 parts of the reef.

Each part of the reef has $\boxed{5}$ fish.

166

You have 20 marbles.

Fill each box with an equal number of marbles to show each division sentence.

$20 \div 4 = \boxed{5}$

$20 \div 5 = \boxed{4}$

$20 \div 10 = \boxed{2}$

Learn Together
Help your child figure out how to fill the boxes. Ask, "Is there another way to share the marbles equally?" (2 boxes with 10 marbles each; 20 boxes with 1 marble each).

167

Measure It!

Who is taller, Sadness or Joy?

You can measure people and objects to find out exactly how tall they are.

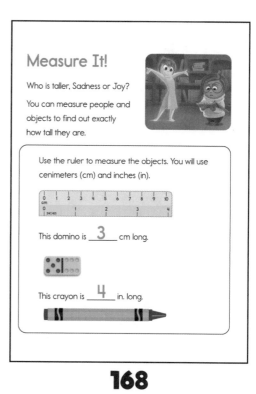

Use the ruler to measure the objects. You will use cenimeters (cm) and inches (in).

This domino is ___3___ cm long.

This crayon is ___4___ in. long.

168

Practice estimating how many feet.

Answers will vary.
Sample answers:

How tall is a giraffe?

A giraffe is about __15__ ft. tall.

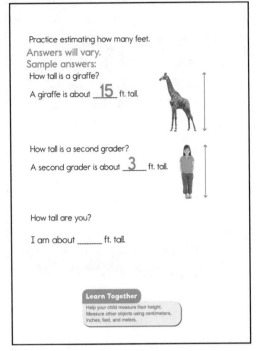

How tall is a second grader?

A second grader is about __3__ ft. tall.

How tall are you?

I am about _____ ft. tall.

Learn Together
Help your child measure their height.
Measure other objects using centimeters,
inches, feet, and meters.

171

Hold It!

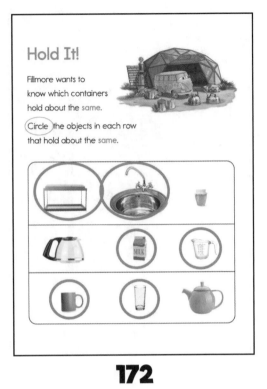

Fillmore wants to
know which containers
hold about the same.

Circle the objects in each row
that hold about the same.

172

Estimate how many glasses of water
each container will hold.

Circle the container that holds the most.

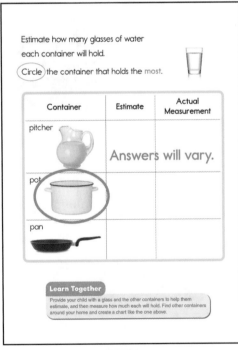

Container	Estimate	Actual Measurement
pitcher		
pot	Answers will vary.	
pan		

Learn Together
Provide your child with a glass and the other containers to help them
estimate, and then measure how much each will hold. Find other containers
around your home and create a chart like the one above.

173

Heavy or Light?

It's the Incredible family!
Who do you think
is the heaviest?

Mr. Incredible

Circle the object in each pair that is heavier.

174

You can use a balance to compare the mass of two objects.

If you put two objects on a balance, how do you know which one is lighter?

The lighter object will be on the side of the scale that is higher than the other side.

Learn Together

Help your child compare the mass of objects using a balance or a kitchen or bathroom scale. Note that your child may not yet have been introduced to units of measurement for mass.

175

How Big?

Estimate the number of squares that cover this picture.

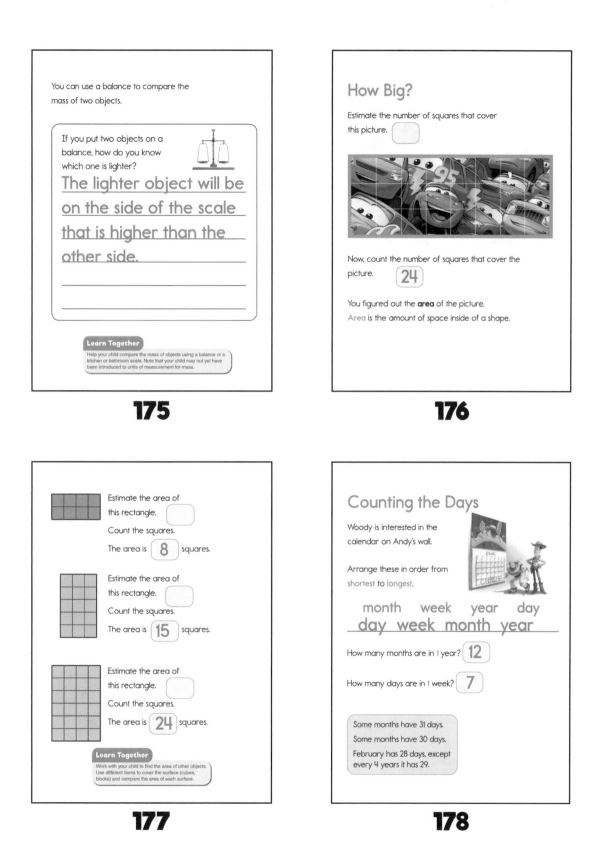

Now, count the number of squares that cover the picture. 24

You figured out the **area** of the picture.
Area is the amount of space inside of a shape.

176

Estimate the area of this rectangle.

Count the squares.

The area is 8 squares.

Estimate the area of this rectangle.

Count the squares.

The area is 15 squares.

Estimate the area of this rectangle.

Count the squares.

The area is 24 squares.

Learn Together

Work with your child to find the area of other objects. Use different items to cover the surface (cubes, blocks) and compare the area of each surface.

177

Counting the Days

Woody is interested in the calendar on Andy's wall.

Arrange these in order from shortest to longest.

month   week   year   day
day   week   month   year

How many months are in 1 year? 12

How many days are in 1 week? 7

Some months have 31 days.
Some months have 30 days.
February has 28 days, except every 4 years it has 29.

178

Time Enough

It's time for Riley to go to bed.

Match each analog clock to the correct digital clock.

180

Shaping Up

Hank can see many shapes when he escapes his tank.

What shapes do you see in this picture?

Complete the table below.

Shape	Draw the Shape	Number of Sides
square		4
rectangle		4
triangle		3
circle		0

182

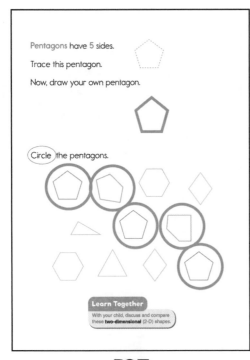

Pentagons have 5 sides.

Trace this pentagon.

Now, draw your own pentagon.

Circle the pentagons.

Learn Together
With your child, discuss and compare these **two-dimensional** (2-D) shapes.

183

Many Sides

Can you find a hexagon in this picture?

Hexagons have 6 sides.

Trace this hexagon.

Now, draw your own hexagon.

Circle the hexagons.

184

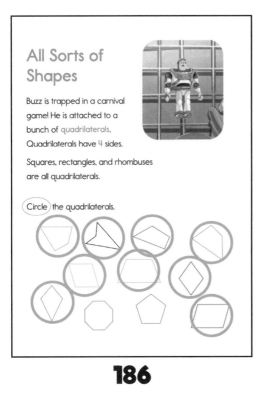

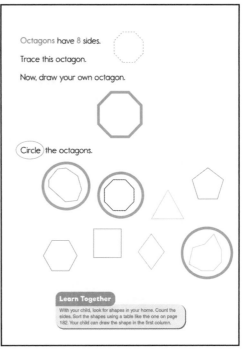

Octagons have 8 sides.

Trace this octagon.

Now, draw your own octagon.

Circle the octagons.

185

All Sorts of Shapes

Buzz is trapped in a carnival game! He is attached to a bunch of quadrilaterals. Quadrilaterals have 4 sides.

Squares, rectangles, and rhombuses are all quadrilaterals.

Circle the quadrilaterals.

186

Complete the table below.

Shape	Draw the Shape	Number of Sides
pentagon		5
hexagon		6
octagon		8
quadrilateral		4

187

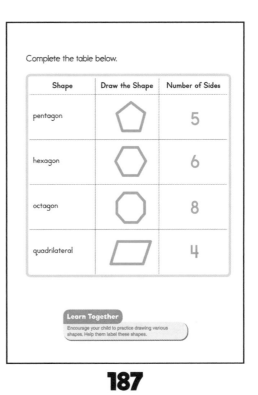

Answers

Shape Fun!

What shapes do you see in this truck?

What shapes make up the truck below? Label the shapes.

triangle
rectangle
circle
square

188

Power Objects

Circle the 3-D objects you see in this picture.

Use these words to name each 3-D object below.

cube   cone   cylinder   sphere

cylinder   cube

sphere   cone

Answers will vary. Sample answer:
Name one of the 3-D objects you circled in the picture.

cylinder

190

Use the clues to answer these riddles.

All my faces are the same and I have 8 vertices.

What am I? __cube__

edge

I have one vertex and can roll.

What am I? __cone__

vertex

I have flat faces and can roll.

What am I? __cylinder__

face

I have no vertices and can roll.

What am I? __sphere__

Learn Together

Help your child create other riddles for **three-dimensional** (3-D) objects. Your child can create 3-D objects using modeling clay or other materials. They can describe and label the objects.

191

In 3-D

Can you find the cones and spheres in this picture?

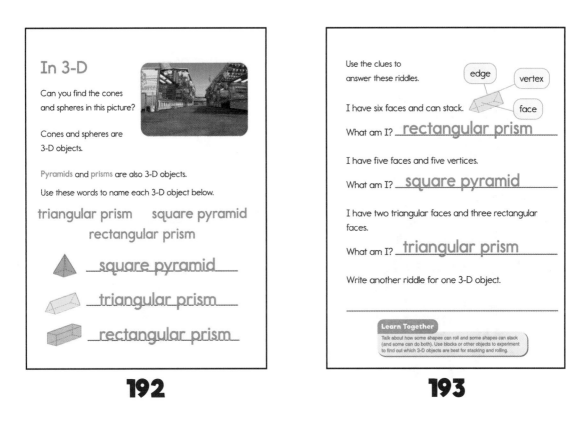

Cones and spheres are 3-D objects.

Pyramids and prisms are also 3-D objects.

Use these words to name each 3-D object below.

triangular prism   square pyramid
rectangular prism

__square pyramid__

__triangular prism__

__rectangular prism__

192

Use the clues to answer these riddles.

edge   vertex   face

I have six faces and can stack.

What am I? __rectangular prism__

I have five faces and five vertices.

What am I? __square pyramid__

I have two triangular faces and three rectangular faces.

What am I? __triangular prism__

Write another riddle for one 3-D object.

_____

Learn Together

Talk about how some shapes can roll and some shapes can stack (and some can do both). Use blocks or other objects to experiment to find out which 3-D objects are best for stacking and rolling.

193

Start at Erica's house.

Walk east along Queen Street.

Turn north on Oak Road. Walk to the end of the street.

Where are you? __hospital__

Write directions from the hospital to the store.

__Walk south on Oak Rd.__
__Turn west on Main St.__
__Walk past Ash Rd.__

Write directions from the community center to the library.

__Walk west on Main St. Walk__
__past Ash Rd.__

Learn Together

Examine the map together. Help your child create a map of your neighborhood. As you work, use phrases such as behind, near, far, and in front of to describe location. Use the map to create directions for another person to follow.

195

What Are the Chances?

Jackson Storm   Chuck Armstrong

Lightning McQueen   Manny Flywheel

Cruz Ramirez

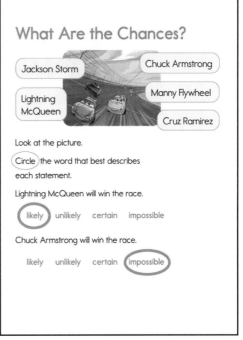

Look at the picture.

Circle the word that best describes each statement.

Lightning McQueen will win the race.

(likely)   unlikely   certain   impossible

Chuck Armstrong will win the race.

likely   unlikely   certain   (impossible)

196

Manny Flywheel will win the race.

likely (unlikely) certain impossible

Chuck Armstrong will finish the race before Jackson Storm.

likely (unlikely) certain impossible

This race will have a winner.

likely unlikely (certain) impossible

Answers will vary. Sample answer:
Write your own **probability** statement about the race.

Lightning McQueen will come
in last place. (Unlikley)

Learn Together

Discuss the meaning of each probability phrase with your child. Encourage them to use one of these phrases as they write a new statement. Play games with spinners or dice to help your child learn about probability.

197

Picturing Numbers

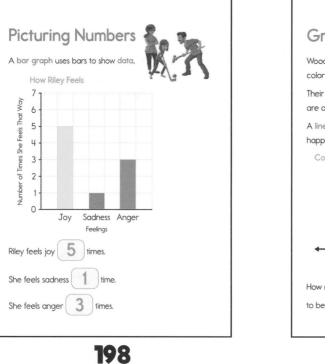

A bar graph uses bars to show data.

How Riley Feels

Riley feels joy [5] times.

She feels sadness [1] time.

She feels anger [3] times.

198

Graph Up

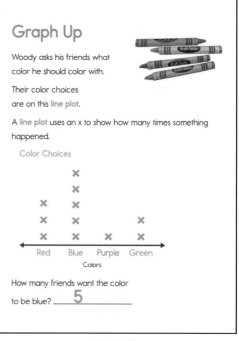

Woody asks his friends what color he should color with.

Their color choices are on this line plot.

A line plot uses an x to show how many times something happened.

Color Choices

How many friends want the color to be blue? ___5___

200

Congratulations

to

_____

for completing this workbook!
Keep up the good work!

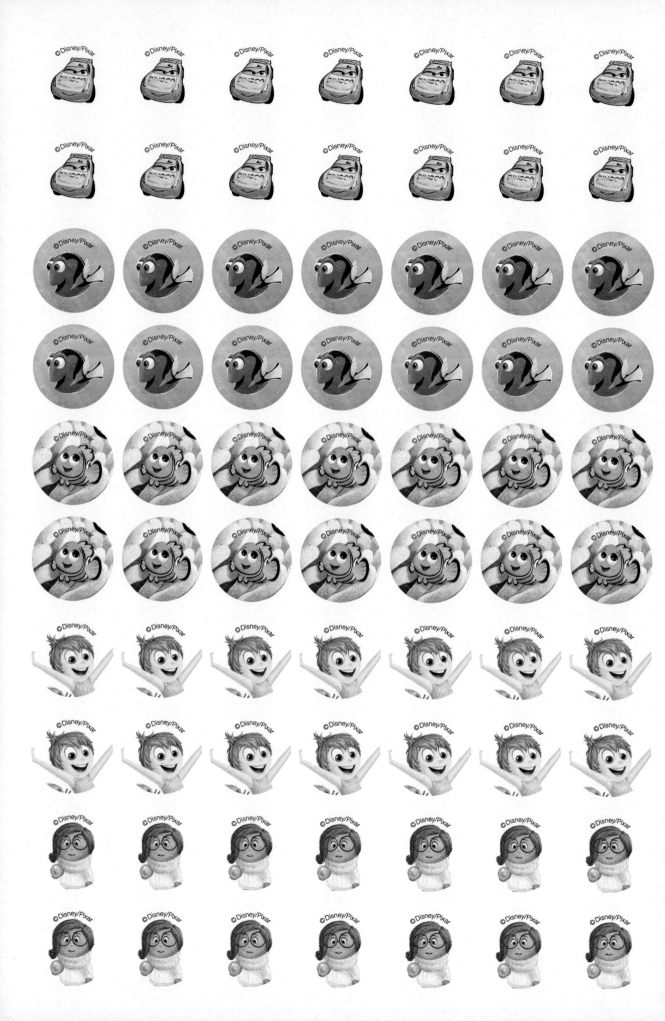